7 BILLION LIVES ARE IN DANGER.
13 STRANGERS WITH TERRIFYING NIGHTMARES.
1 ENEMY WILL STOP AT NOTHING TO DESTROY US ALL.

MY NAME IS SAM.
I AM ONE OF THE LAST THIRTEEN.
OUR BATTLE CONTINUES . . .

This one is for Sam. Sam, if you annoy me . . . —JP.

Scholastic Canada Ltd.
604 King Street West, Toronto, Ontario M5V 1E1, Canada

Scholastic Inc.
557 Broadway, New York, NY 10012, USA

Scholastic Australia Pty Limited
PO Box 579, Gosford, NSW 2250, Australia

Scholastic New Zealand Limited
Private Bag 94407, Botany, Manukau 2163, New Zealand

Scholastic Children's Books
Euston House, 24 Eversholt Street, London NW1 1DB, UK

www.scholastic.ca

MIX
Paper from
responsible sources
FSC® C004071

Library and Archives Canada Cataloguing in Publication
Phelan, James, 1979-, author
    4 / James Phelan.
(The last thirteen ; book 10)
Issued in print and electronic formats.
ISBN 978-1-4431-3393-7 (pbk.).--ISBN 978-1-4431-3394-4 (html)
    I. Title. II. Title: Four. III. Series: Phelan, James, 1979- .
Last thirteen ; bk. 10.
PZ7.P52Fo 2014   j823'.92   C2014-901814-2
                                          C2014-901815-0

First published by Scholastic Australia in 2014. This edition published by Scholastic Canada Ltd. in 2014.
Text copyright © 2014 by James Phelan. Illustrations & design copyright © 2014 by Scholastic Australia.
Illustrations by Chad Mitchell. Design by Nicole Stofberg.

Cover photography: Blueprint © istockphoto.com/Adam Korzekwa; Parkour Tic-Tac © istockphoto.com/Willie B. Thomas; Climbing wall © istockphoto.com/microgen; Leonardo da Vinci (Sepia) © istockphoto.com/pictore; Gears © istockphoto.com/-Oxford-; Mechanical blueprint © istockphoto.com/teekid; Circuit board © istockphoto.com/Björn Meyer; Map © istockphoto.com/alengo; Grunge drawing © istockphoto.com/aleksandar velasevic; World map © istockphoto.com/Maksim Pasko; Internet © istockphoto.com/Andrey Prokhorov; Inside clock © istockphoto.com/LdF; Space galaxy © istockphoto.com/Sergii Tsololo; Sunset © istockphoto.com/Joakim Leroy; Blue flare © istockphoto.com/YouraPechkin; Global communication © istockphoto.com/chadive samanthakamani; Earth satellites © istockphoto.com/Alexey Popov; Girl portrait © istockphoto.com/peter zelei; Student & board © istockphoto.com/zhang bo; Young man serious © istockphoto.com/Jacob Wackerhausen; Portrait man © istockphoto.com/Alina Solovyova-Vincent; Sad expression © istockphoto.com/Shelly Perry; Content man © istockphoto.com/drbimages; Pensive man © istockphoto.com/Chuck Schmidt; Black and pink © istockphoto.com/blackwaterimages; Punk Girl © istockphoto.com/Kuzma; Woman escaping © Jose antonio Sanchez reyes/Photos.com; Young running man © Tatiana Belova/Photos.com; Gears clock © Jupiterimages/Photos.com; Woman portrait © Nuzza/Shutterstock.com; Explosions © Leigh Prather/Dreamstime.com; Landscape blueprints © Firebrandphotography/Dreamstime.com; Jump over wall © Ammentorp/Dreamstime.com; Mountains, CAN © Akadiusz Iwanicki/Dreamstime.com; Sphinx Bucegi © Adrian Nicolae/Dreamstime.com; Big mountains © Hoptrop/Dreamstime.com; Sunset mountains © Pklimenko/Dreamstime.com; Mountains lake © Jan Mika/Dreamstime.com; Blue night sky © Mack2happy/Dreamstime.com; Old writing © Empire331/Dreamstime.com; Young man © Shuen Ho Wang/Dreamstime.com; Abstract cells © Sur/Dreamstime.com; Helicopter © Evren Kalinbacak/Dreamstime.com; Aeroplane © Rgbe/Dreamstime.com; Phrenology illustration © Mcarrel/Dreamstime.com; Abstract interior © Sur/Dreamstime.com; Papyrus © Cebreros/Dreamstime.com; Blue shades © Mohamed Osama/Dreamstime.com; Blue background © Matusciac/Dreamstime.com; Sphinx and Pyramid © Dan Breckwoldt/Dreamstime.com; Blue background2 © Cammeraydave/Dreamstime.com; Abstract shapes © Lisa Mckown/Dreamstime.com; Yellow Field © Simon Greig/Dreamstime.com; Blue background3 © Sergey Skrebnev/Dreamstime.com; Blue eye © Richard Thomas/Dreamstime.com; Abstract landscape © Crazy80frog/Dreamstime.com; Rameses II © Jose I. Soto/Dreamstime.com; Helicopter © Sculpies/Dreamstime.com; Vitruvian man © Cornelius20/Dreamstime.com; Scarab beetle © Charon/Dreamstime.com; Eye of Horus © Charon/Dreamstime.com; Handsome male portrait © DigitalHand Studio/Shutterstock.com; Teen girl © CREATISTA/Shutterstock.com; Angkor Wat in afternoon light © Bernardo Ertl/Dreamstime.com; Cremation temple in Phnom Penh Cambodia © Jackmalipan/Dreamstime.com; Rooftop view of Phnom Penh, Cambodia © Thor Jorgen Udvang/Dreamstime.com; Phnom Penh Cambodia map © Robert Bayer/Dreamstime.com; Royal palace in Phnom Penh © Ckchiu/Dreamstime.com; Reliefs-Phnom Penh, Cambodia © Rfoxphoto/Dreamstime.com; Silver pagoda close-up, Phnom Penh, Cambodia © Shariff Che\' Lah/Dreamstime.com; Garden Phnom Penh-Cambodia (hdr) © Martin Roeder/Dreamstime.com; Phnom Penh skyline-Cambodia © Rfoxphoto/Dreamstime.com; Angkor © Zoom-zoom/Dreamstime.com; Angkor2 © Zoom-zoom/Dreamstime.com; Angkor Wat bas-reliefs © Alexey Stiop/Dreamstime.com; Angkor Ta Prohm temple © Bidouze Stéphane/Dreamstime.com; Angkor Wat © Achim Baqué/Dreamstime.com; Angkor Wat © David Davis/Dreamstime.com; Angkor Wat © Andrewblue/Dreamstime.com; Angkor Thom © Skouatroulio/Dreamstime.com; Independence monument in Phnom Penh, Cambodia © Jackmalipan/Dreamstime.com; Airport on Pohnpei Island, Micronesia © Sgoodwin4813/Dreamstime.com; World War II Era Japanese guns on Pohnpei Island © Sgoodwin4813/Dreamstime.com; Preah Khan in Cambodia © Chenyun Fan/Dreamstime.com; Stone doorways at Bayon temple, Angkor Wat, Cambodia © Jjiroy/Dreamstime.com; Red stone carving of the Banteay Srei temple © Tourthatree/Dreamstime.com; Stone alley to weathered temple door © Til5/Dreamstime.com; Aerial view of Micronesia Islands © Richard Brooks/Dreamstime.com; Divers descending © Eric Lemar/Dreamstime.com.
Internal photography: p12, Open file © istockphoto.com/Roel Smart; p12, Polaroid frame © istockphoto.com/hohos; p145, Table © Dr. Lee T. Shapiro, Director Morehead Planetarium University of North Carolina, Chapel Hill.

6 5 4 3 2 1   Printed in Canada 121   14 15 16 17 18 19

THE LAST
THIRTEEN

BOOK TEN

JAMES PHELAN

Scholastic Canada Ltd.
Toronto New York London Auckland Sydney
Mexico City New Delhi Hong Kong Buenos Aires

PREVIOUSLY

Sam is once again rescued by Arianna and they flee from the fire engulfing the Hypnos' dream-stealing facility. Sam is amazed at the chance they get to steal back the Gears from his sinister captor, Hans.

Sam's next nightmare reveals Issey, a pro-gamer from Japan, as the next of the last 13. Sam wakes from his dream more disturbed than ever, not only by visions of Solaris, but monstrous flesh-eating beasts.

Struggling with feelings of helplessness, Eva's thoughts turn to the upcoming Dreamer Doors Competition—the best chance the Academy has to find where Solaris has hidden his Gears.

Alex and Shiva remain captive in a New York apartment, fitted with explosive wristbands to prevent escape. They eventually manage to deactivate the bombs with seconds to spare, in the process uncovering Matrix's plot to hijack the Dreamer Doors.

Tobias and Sam realize their attempt to secretly travel to Japan was unsuccessful when they learn that Stella and her Agents have also arrived in Tokyo. They go to meet Issey as planned, but must run from the horrific scene at the stadium to the safe house belonging to Issey's wise Dreamer grandfather, Kaga.

Eva is surprised to find herself selected on the team for the Dreamer Doors with Zara and Xavier, and becomes preoccupied by Jedi's discovery that she too will very likely be one of the last 13.

Sam wakes to the shocking realization that Solaris is inside Kaga's house. At Kaga's urging, Sam and Issey escape out the window to fulfil their combined destiny, leaving the old man to fight Solaris alone.

Shaken by their decision to leave Kaga, Issey and Sam travel with Issey's Enterprise surrogates and Tobias to the mysterious Ghost Island to find Issey's Gear. There they are stalked by shadowy beasts, Stella's Agents and Solaris himself. In a shocking display of evil, Solaris turns on his own followers to take the Gear, destroying all in his path and leaving Sam for dead in the stormy sea.

SAM'S NIGHTMARE

The bright orange sunlight shines off the tops of ancient stone buildings. Birds sing as they dart by me. Green jungle stretches below me, a vast blanket of trees swaying with the breeze, interrupted only by waterways and relics. This is paradise. And it feels like I'm floating over it, flying—seeing everything all at once.

"Sam!"

I'm on the ground now, standing in an elevated clearing in front of one of the immense temple palaces that surround me. I turn around to look for the voice, but I'm alone.

"Sam!" the voice says again. I spin around, scanning full circle.

Suddenly, I see a tiny figure emerge from the trees below.

Eva.

She starts running toward me. I look around again, panicked that some threat is waiting—like I am—but there is no one else. My panic makes the beautiful sculptures in the ornately carved stone tower feel somehow dark and menacing.

I watch Eva as she nears. She breaks into a smile, and then she is laughing.

Eva's not afraid, she's–*happy*.

"Sam," Eva says, "come down!"

I clamber down the rough stone stairs and Eva crashes into me.

"Hey, you're crushing me!" I say, laughing, and Eva releases me from her hug.

"What are you doing here?" I ask.

"I'm with them," Eva says, looking back over her shoulder to the trees where she's just come from.

I watch as a group of people appear in the distance. They run toward us too.

"Is that . . . ?"

"Yes," Eva replies.

"And . . ."

"Yes," Eva says. "We're all here."

I smile as the rest of the last 13 rush toward us. They all look happy.

First comes Alex, waving like crazy.

It feels like forever since I've seen him.

Gabriella, the Italian pop star, follows him with Xavier. Next comes the French art student, Zara, with Rapha from Brazil. Right behind them are Maria from Cuba, Cody from the States and Arianna, the feisty Russian gymnast. Issey, the pro-gamer from Japan, is at the back. And then I notice someone else.

"Who's that?" I ask Eva.

"That's Poh," Eva says.

"Poh . . . the next Dreamer?"

Eva nods.

"But it can't be, can it? *I'm* supposed to find him," I say.

Eva shrugs and stays silent.

"I'm supposed to be the one who finds the last 13," I repeat, my panic returning. "And if I'm dreaming of the next Dreamer now, then who else can see . . ."

No answer.

"Eva?"

I turn to Eva, but she's gone. I look back toward the group, but they're gone too.

The tall grass that stretches away from where I stand seems to whisper in the breeze. The lush jungle trees sway in unison. The ancient building to my back is casting a longer shadow over the rock-paved court. The sun is going down. But fast—too fast. Like I'm watching a time-delay sequence. I know *he* will be here. I know he is coming.

I close my eyes.

Wake up, wake up, wake up . . .

I open my eyes to a new scene.

I stare, confused, before realizing—

I haven't woken up.

This is not a new scene. I'm in the same place, but seeing it from a far different viewpoint.

I'm up high now, above the trees. I'm standing at the very top of the temple spire. Somehow I know now where I am.

Cambodia.

At the temple of Angkor Wat, to be precise.

On top of the highest tower.

I look out over the sprawling complex and can see for the first time the majesty of the place—the trees, the grass lawns, the surrounding moat.

I know I'm in a dream, that this may be where I have to go next. I sit and wait—listening, watching.

But nothing happens. Time does not seem to pass. Birds fly, clouds move, leaves rustle, but it feels like everything is on a repetitive loop—nothing is going forward.

Eventually, I close my eyes.

When I open them, things will change.

Bill is standing there. My best friend from my old high school. My best friend, who died in the house fire. We are at the temple forecourt.

"Hi," I say. "Are you OK?"

"Of course," he replies.

"Why are you here? *How* are you here?"

"I'm in your dream, Sam."

"Right . . ."

"You're making this happen," Bill says.

"I am?"

"Yes, because you know something is not right. You're in trouble. You should wake up."

"I guess, but I don't feel worried anymore." I look around at the scenery—the birds still flying, uniform clouds are inching across the horizon, the trees swaying in the same unchanging rhythm.

The loop continues.

"Wake up, Sam."

"But I need information. Poh was here."

"Not now—later."

"But what about you?"

The birds freeze mid-flight.

I feel a shiver run through me. The shudder ripples down my spine like an electrical spark as a dark shadow is cast over me.

Bill turns to me. "It's too late, Sam. You couldn't save me then, and you can't save me now."

What? No!

Bill laughs, distorting his face into an ugly grimace. "You're always going to be too late, *boy*."

Boy?

Is this Solaris?

"You're not Bill!" I jump to my feet and push him away.

"But Sam, please, help me!" Bill suddenly looks like himself again, now scared and reaching for me.

What do I do?

But there is nothing I can do. It *is* too late. The flames are already surrounding us as Bill grabs my hand, frantically looking for an escape, but there is none.

I close my eyes as I hang onto him. Knowing it's coming does not lessen the horror as the huge fireball erupts and I hear Bill's screams mingling with mine as we—

Burn.

SAM

Sam floated on his back in a dark, angry sea. When he opened his eyes, staring upwardly in a daze, he could see a black sky, empty of stars. Rain fell. All he could hear was the white noise of water in the storm.

How long have I been here, floating like this?

Dreaming.

The memory of his nightmare brought Sam back to life and he sputtered out water as a small wave crashed over him. He didn't fight the rise and fall of the sea, instead trying to relax, going with it, like a tiny cork bobbing in the middle of the ocean. His back ached from lying on the piece of debris, his arms trailing in the water.

Where am I?

In the darkness, there was a soft glow over the waves, red and orange, reminding him again of the inferno of his dream. He forced himself upright and the plank was pulled away on the waves.

Great.

He began to tread water, looking around, searching—

His world was suddenly illuminated, a blinding, pure

white light washing over him, as if all the lights of the world had been turned on in the blink of an eye. He could not see anything through the whiteness and found it impossible to locate its source. Instead he tried to swim in what he thought was the direction of the glow. Then, just as quickly, he was plunged into darkness again.

"Argh!"

A large piece of wood hit him in the shoulder, gliding over a breaking wave like a surfboard. It was ablaze at one end. Sam clung to it, exhausted, letting it carry his weight.

The wooden plank looked like it was a side panel from a boat.

A boat?

I'm in Japan—Solaris attacked us. Issey . . . Tobias . . .

"Tobias!" Sam called into the night. He began screaming Tobias' name, over and over again until he was hoarse. It was useless. His voice was drowned out in the noise of the raging storm and the sea.

It's useless . . . useless . . .

Sam turned the word over in his head as he floated for a while, resigned, clinging to the plank of wood from the wrecked fishing boat. With no other point of reference, he kicked off once again in the direction of the faint orange glow he now assumed was the wreck of the boat, still alight.

Something big bumped into him, the impact forcing his makeshift wooden life raft from his grasp.

Sam splashed in the water trying to regain his balance. There was movement around him. A black shape was moving toward him in the darkness of the night. It was fast, glimmering like a huge fish, or dolphin, or . . . *shark*.

Sam turned and swam back in the other direction as fast as his tired arms would propel him through the water.

He felt something grab onto him.

"ARGH!" Sam yelled out as he tried to kick away.

A light hit him, brilliant white as before, from above. This time, it was constant, burning brightly down on him.

A new noise could be heard. A familiar, mechanical churning, growing louder.

A helicopter!

Its searchlight was fixed on Sam, and in the bright channel of light he could see a silhouette—a figure, wearing goggles and scuba gear.

Sam gave a relieved smile.

No shark attacks for me today.

The diver put a harness over Sam's head and under his arms. He flashed Sam a quick thumbs up and Sam replied with the same. Together they were winched up into the sky.

As they boarded the helicopter, Sam saw the Japanese crewman who had manned the searchlight. He helped Sam out of the harness.

I guess the Professor got the Japanese government to help.

"Thanks!" Sam shouted out to him and the diver over the roar of the engine and the sea below. He looked out the open side door, down to the flaming wreck of what was left of the boat.

Solaris did that . . .

The last Dreamer, Issey, and his parents had been on the boat with him, Tobias too.

"Did you already pick up the others?" Sam asked.

None of the crew answered him.

Instead of searching for more survivors, Sam could feel the helicopter dip its nose, turning, before it started to pick up speed through the air. The crewman slid the side door shut against the storm.

"We can't leave!" Sam pleaded with them. "My friends are somewhere down there, you can't leave them behind!"

The men said nothing in response. The diver took off his scuba gear and began to look over Sam, breaking out a first-aid pack.

Sam collapsed to the floor, too exhausted to protest. "We have to go back," he said in a quiet voice to the diver, who was wrapping a tight bandage around Sam's leg, crimson blood oozing from a cut. "We have to go back . . ."

ALEX

Alex looked out over the Pacific Ocean and swallowed hard at the sight. They were off the south coast of Hawaii. In one way, Alex was enjoying his first time at sea. But beneath the feeling of adventure and usefulness, the voyage also had all the hallmarks of a dream gone wrong.

It's not that I hate water. It's just the thought of going under . . .

His hands became clammy with sweat and his breathing got faster as he imagined himself sinking into the vast, bottomless water.

"Beautiful, isn't it?" Hans said in his sharp German accent.

Alex didn't answer. He gripped the handrail tighter while instinctively leaning his body as far back as he could. Shock therapy. He swallowed again at rising bile.

You're just seasick. Control your fear or it will control you.

"Did you read what I prepared for you?" Hans asked.

Alex nodded. He had. He'd read the reports on the flight from New York—lots of them. The reports made it clear that someone had been watching Alex for a while now.

There were photos of him with Phoebe at the Enterprise headquarters, and running back and forth with Shiva working on the Tesla dream coils in New York. Hans had somehow been able to get his hands on a lot of data from both the Academy and the Enterprise. It surprised him just how much information Hans had gained access to and how much he really knew.

S'pose money really can buy you everything . . .

There were reports on the last 13 Dreamers found so far and some false leads—photos of other teenagers, red crosses drawn through the pictures. And Alex rifled through pages of data on Sam, some going back to before they were even picked up by the Enterprise.

One report that Alex had eagerly read, which had the original source blacked out at the top, speculated about Alex's own dreams. It expanded on what the Director and Professor had told him earlier—that his dreamwaves shared unique patterns with the other known last 13 Dreamers and concluded that he was likely to be one of the last 13.

Alex couldn't help but feel a surge of excitement pulse through his body when he read that particular report.

But when will I dream of my Gear? And why didn't the Enterprise show me all this information before?

Alex thought back over how he came to be here. Despite the way Hans had appeared, looking set to take Alex hostage, Alex had agreed to go along with Hans and his crew—it seemed like as logical a next step as any. How else could they find out what was going on in the mind of one of their enemies? And the fact that Hans had also been holding da Vinci's journal, which must have come from someone at the Academy, made up Alex's mind in an instant.

Man, Mom must be totally freaking out . . . and I'm pretty sure Shiva's going to be mad being left like that in New York.

Hans had continued to sell his side of the story to Alex from that first moment—*"Alex, what we've seen of you over the last weeks is extraordinary. You are a gifted Dreamer, and I have the means to allow you to reach your full potential,"* he had said to him, and Alex had been curious. And now, after listening to all that Hans had to say, and reading through the reports, Alex was convinced.

I'm going to be one of the last 13. Maybe even the last Dreamer . . . the one at the very end.

Hans broke into Alex's daydream as he said, "Did you notice anything special about this ship after we left the docks in Hawaii?"

"Ah . . ." Alex looked around, "not really."

"How about now?" Hans said, touching his watch.

"Um, no, you've lost me," Alex said, glancing around. The ship seemed just like any other.

OK, not that I've been on many billionaires' boats . . .

"You may be familiar with this Stealth technology," Hans said. "The Academy jet had the same capabilities, I believe."

Alex stiffened but said nothing.

"It's always good to have," Hans continued, undeterred, "in case we have to hide. And this little beauty can disappear altogether at the touch of a button." Hans beamed with pride.

"Are you *expecting* we'll have to hide?" Alex asked, trying to act coolly in response to this information.

Hans shrugged. "It always pays to be prepared, Alex."

"For Solaris?"

"Him, the others," Hans said smugly. "But mostly I find it's best to be prepared for anything." He started to walk down the deck toward the main cabin. "Why don't you come inside?" Hans said. "Our chef has put on lunch."

The ship was named the *Ra* and the main area was a large open-plan living area with windows all around. The space was furnished with plush leather couches at one end, expensive-looking chairs clustered around a marble table in the middle and a long, well-stocked bar that glistened with polished crystal and glassware. It could have been a five-star hotel suite anywhere in the world. But every time Alex looked out a window, he was reminded where they were—sitting inside a tiny speck on top of a bottomless ocean.

The dining table was filled with platters of food, the likes of which Alex had not seen since his mom had taken him to an all-you-can-eat buffet for his last birthday.

Gotta call my mom . . . Alex thought as he sat down. *After I eat.*

Opposite him was the only other passenger on the *Ra* besides himself and Hans and the ship's staff and security guys. He had already been on the boat when they'd gotten to the marina in Oahu a few hours earlier. Alex had not had a chance to speak to him.

The man was reading through notes and a stack of books, constantly checking and rechecking, and making more notes. He looked like a librarian, or even like the guy who wrote Alex's favourite series of novels.

Man, what was that author's name again . . . ?

"Alex, this is Dr. Kader," Hans said. "The world's leading Egyptologist and, through expertise known only in certain circles, our greatest Dream Gate scholar."

Dr. Kader looked up from his notes and smiled at Alex over his reading glasses perched at the end of his nose. "Call me Ahmed," he said.

"It's, ah, nice to meet you, Ahmed," Alex said, and he shook his hand. "Hang on, Ahmed *Kader*? Aren't you the guy that sold out the Academy to that Mac dude?"

Hans could see Alex's growing irritation as he made the connection. "Alex, Ahmed is the most reliable source we have on the Dream Gate—" he started to say.

"Well, I know a few 'reliable sources' myself," Alex countered, cutting him off, "and they all told me this guy's got no loyalty to anyone."

SAM

Sam leaned wearily against the pillows and looked around the small hospital room. He hadn't seen any other patients as he was wheeled in on the stretcher, and hadn't seen any since. The medical staff had looked him over, cleaned and patched up a few cuts and grazes. A heart-rate monitor was connected to his chest and the machine beeped rhythmically next to the narrow bed. Nurses popped in and out, busy, checking on him regularly.

The anxiety he felt about his missing friends only increased as he thought back to his dream.

Cambodia. The Dreamer's name is Poh.

I have to get out of here.

But something in the dream wasn't right . . .

The beeping from the monitor began to get faster and louder, and a doctor shuffled into the room to read the screen display.

"Please," Sam said to the doctor as he pressed the buttons to cut the noise. "My friends. They might still be out there, in the water."

The doctor looked at him.

"The water—the sea, where they found me," Sam said. "Do you understand? I was on a boat, near Ghost Island."

The doctor smiled sympathetically, but his expression remained blank.

"There were four other people on that boat, they might still be out there," Sam said. "I've been here for hours. You need to send help!"

"No, we don't," a voice said. It belonged to a middle-aged man dressed in a dark suit with well-groomed silver hair. He stood in the doorway, watching. At the sight of him, the doctor gave a small bow and walked hurriedly over to the man. The two spoke in hushed tones, the doctor then bowed again and left. The man looked to Sam and walked over.

Is that . . . ?

Sam had seen this man on the news as he had flicked through the TV channels while lying in the hospital bed. It was the Prime Minister of Japan, Yutaka Hashimoto. He also knew of him from a school research project on a G20 summit. He'd done the assignment with Bill. A week later, his friend had died in the fire.

Bill was in my dream. The fire, Solaris . . .

"So, Sam," the Prime Minister said, snapping him out of his daze. "I am very pleased to see you alive and well. We feared the worst."

"We?" Sam said hopefully.

The Prime Minister looked over his shoulder.

Tobias and Issey were standing in the doorway, smiling.

"Where are your parents?" Sam asked Issey, after they'd all greeted each other.

"They are in a civilian hospital," Issey said. "It is OK, Sam. They will be fine."

"Good," Sam said, exhaling a deep breath. "Wait, a civilian hospital? Then . . . where am I?"

It was the Prime Minister who answered Sam's question. "Sam," he said, "you are in a special government medical centre," he replied. "One of the safest and most secret places available to us."

"The Prime Minister has stepped in to help us, Sam," Issey said.

The older man smiled and nodded. "The least I could do," he said. "I am only sorry that I could not have intervened sooner at the island."

"Thank you for everything you have done," Sam said. He looked to Tobias. "I've had my next dream, I know where I have to go."

"Rest, Sam," Tobias said. "We can talk about it later."

"No," Sam said, sitting up. "I'm ready to go, now."

The Prime Minister smiled. "I, too, am a Dreamer, Sam. And I knew this day would come for me," he said. "If you are well enough, then let us go now. Even here, your presence may be discovered. We must leave. Please, follow me."

Sam started to get out of the bed but Tobias looked uncertain.

"Are you sure you feel up to it?" Tobias said.

"Yep," Sam said, putting both feet on the floor. "Just you watch what happens to someone if they try to stop me."

"The doctor has given Sam a clean bill of health," the Prime Minister said. "And I can make sure you get to where you need to go."

"Thank you," Tobias said, seeming reassured. "We will gladly take you up on that offer."

Sam was already up and pulling out the new Stealth Suit that he'd spied hanging in the wardrobe.

"Nice one," he said. "Thanks, Tobias." Then he paused, looking at everyone in the room.

"Ah, guys, a little privacy?"

They rode in the Prime Minister's limousine, its heavily tinted windows shielding them from the outside world, a motorcade of police surrounding them.

"When I was briefed about the events out on Ghost Island last night, I knew immediately what was really happening. I knew what you were here for," Mr. Hashimoto said, his large gold-rimmed glasses glinting on his friendly face, "because long ago, I had a dream that I would be here, like this, to help you. I did not know the details, only that I would be needed to help a special Dreamer."

"How long ago was this dream?" Tobias asked.

"When I was about their age," he said, gesturing to Sam and Issey. "I knew that it was my destiny."

"Thank you," Sam said.

"It has been my pleasure," Mr. Hashimoto said. "But, I must say, I fear that you will need all the help that you can get. And more help than I can offer alone."

Sam looked to the others, confused.

"I will talk to my counterparts," Mr. Hashimoto said. "The other world leaders. Some are Dreamers too, of course, and already understand. But the time has now come for everyone to know why the world is coming undone—the true reason for the unrest and destruction that is increasing and spreading globally."

"What could they do to help?" Sam asked.

"You would be surprised," Mr. Hashimoto said. "When people unite, when they come together, anything can be achieved."

"Are you suggesting going public?" Tobias asked. "The Dreamer Council has debated this for years—for decades—and have always reached the same conclusion. It won't work."

"The time for talk is over," Mr. Hashimoto said. "The time for secrecy is far behind us. We need to get you, Sam, in front of the leaders of the world to tell your story. That will galvanize support in all corners. That will get the world behind you, as it needs to be."

"*My* story?" Sam said. "I don't even know what my story is."

Mr. Hashimoto smiled. "Of course you do. It is *our* story."

"And you think that will help?" Sam said, his tone still doubtful. He wasn't sure if speaking in front of the public could really be that useful.

Won't everyone just think I'm crazy? And how can it help if people recognize me everywhere I go?

"With a big enough audience, yes, I think so." Mr. Hashimoto nodded. "It will take me a little time to organize, a day or two, but I think I have the audience in mind."

Sam looked to Tobias, deep in thought, considering what the Prime Minister was saying.

"I thought Dreamers had to operate in secret?" Issey said.

"Yes, in a sense, although secret is not really the right word," Tobias replied. "It's just worked that way over the years—we have never spoken publicly about who we are, but we haven't hidden it either. We just let the world make its own assumptions."

"I thought we were laying low now," Sam said, "to get away from Stella and everyone else."

"Sometimes the best defence . . ." Mr. Hashimoto said.

"Is a good offence," Tobias finished for him. "I think

you are right, Prime Minister. Making our mission public will put more pressure on them than us. The world will be watching them as much as us, if not more."

"Good. I will make the plans," Mr. Hashimoto said. "And please call me Yutaka, my friends. We are fighting shoulder to shoulder now."

"OK, I will let the Professor know in the meantime. Please let me know what you organize," Tobias said. He then paused and looked out the window of the speeding car. "By the way, where exactly are we headed now?"

Yutaka smiled. "A place I think you need to see."

EVA

Eva was leaving her Dreamer history class at the London campus of the Academy when she was stopped in her tracks by a group of hysterical students. She heard the commotion before she saw it. It seemed as though half the school were running toward the common room, all talking loudly and at once.

"What is it?" Eva asked Zara, catching up with her as she rushed by.

"The Four Corners Competition," Zara replied. "Haven't you heard?"

"Heard what?"

They both stopped. The other students, still streaming toward the common room, navigated around them.

"It's the team from the South-East quadrant," Zara said, catching her breath. "They were headed to the tournament and there was an accident."

Eva gasped. "What kind of accident?"

"I'm not sure. But, I hear that—well, I don't think they made it."

They both walked sombrely to the common room. Eva

looked over to where the students had massed around the TV screens.

"I think they will postpone the competition," Zara said. "I mean, we are supposed to start tomorrow, against a team from each quadrant, and now with this . . ."

"They can't!" Eva said desperately, looking at her friend. "We need to go. Our dreams can maybe find the Gears Solaris has—it's the only chance we will get. Sam is depending on us."

"Eva," a voice said.

She turned around.

Lora was standing there. She looked sad. "Get the others, quick as you can," she said. "We have a meeting in the Professor's office."

The Professor confirmed the worst—the chartered plane carrying the team from the South-East quadrant came down after takeoff, and from early investigations of the wreckage it looked like there were suspicious circumstances.

"Any survivors?" Eva asked.

Lora shook her head. Xavier and Zara, Eva's teammates for the upcoming competition, looked on, both shocked and silent.

"Who could have done this?" Eva asked.

"We suspect it might be the same people who shot down your helicopter, Eva," Lora said. "Those who want the Dream Gate never found."

Lora looked to the Professor, who nodded grimly.

"The Egyptian Guardians," Eva whispered, instinctively gazing out the Professor's office window at a group of Guardians patrolling the grounds. "How could they do this? Blowing up the Dream Stele in New York was bad enough, but at least no one was killed. But this . . ."

"These Guardians believe it is their role to protect the world. They feel justified in their behaviour," Lora said. "It is what they have been trained to believe above everything—that the secret location of the Dream Gate is *never* to be revealed."

The Professor sighed. "At least we now know about Sam and Tobias."

Eva turned around immediately to look at the Professor, her heart racing. "What? What do we know?"

"Don't worry, they're fine. I have just had word from the Japanese Prime Minister."

Wow, way to go to the top, Sam.

SAM

"This room is called Yume Uchū," Yutaka said. "The English translation would be something like, 'the Dream Universe.'"

Sam looked around the chamber in awe. The small, windowless room had been perfectly carved into solid granite. There were crystals embedded all over the dark stone, reflecting like stars in their flashlight beams, almost as if the four of them were standing within the night sky.

"Well, I can understand the name," Sam sighed in wonder.

"How long has this place been here?" Issey asked. "When was it carved out like this, I mean?"

"The first reference to the Yume Uchū is from Emperor Jimmu's reign," Yutaka said, "and for the two and a half thousand years since, a select group of samurai have fought to keep this a secret. This secrecy has kept it safe."

"And your present-day Guardians," Tobias said, "they continue to protect it?"

"Yes," Yutaka replied, "they do."

"Who made it?" Sam asked, running his hand along the smooth wall and feeling a surge run through him.

"We do not know for certain," Yutaka replied, "but organic material extracted from the stone surface has been carbon dated to around fifteen thousand years ago."

"Fifteen *thousand*?" Sam said.

"Approximately, yes."

"Someone made this *that* long ago?" Issey asked, stunned.

Yutaka nodded.

"But, this is . . ." Sam's voice trailed off as he looked around. "It's amazing to think that something so incredible has been here so long." He looked to Tobias, who was inspecting the walls.

"They call it the myth of progress," Tobias said. "The idea that today we know more than those before us. Could we make this room now? Probably. But would it be any easier than fifteen thousand years ago? Perhaps, I'm not sure. Sometimes humanity forgets, over time, how they built things."

"How to build this room," Yutaka said, a wise grin on his face.

"How to build the pyramids," Tobias added.

"How to best master the subconscious world," Yutaka said, and the two older men looked at each other.

"The dream world," Sam said. "That's what you mean, right?"

Tobias and Yutaka nodded.

"Who knows about this place?" Sam asked.

"Only the Guardians who brought us here," Yutaka said.

"Your bodyguard and driver are both Guardians?" Sam said.

"Yes. The Guardians here have long acted differently to other Guardians elsewhere in the world. Here, they have always worked for our leaders, our modern political and royal figures and all the way back to the shoguns and emperors of long ago. This room has been a sacred space for as long as we remember."

"The knowledge is passed between them?" Tobias said.

"Yes," Yutaka said, "that is the way it has always been, to keep it safe."

"So it's not—vandalized?" Issey asked.

"Or used for other purposes," Sam replied. He thought back to their car ride here. Special blacked-out windows had been activated for the last hour of driving, so that they could not see the exact location of the Dream Universe. The local Guardians wanted this secret kept.

"I've seen something like this before," Tobias said, "in Mexico. A kind of dream room. Your name for it is good."

"Wow . . ." Sam inspected the stone walls closely again. They were so smooth, all leading toward an inverse pyramid in the centre that came down from the roof, shaped from some sort of dark crystal. "There are more of these chambers around the world?"

"Yes," Tobias answered, "there's also one in Chile, and another on Easter Island that I have read about, and perhaps a couple of other locations that have been destroyed."

"Who would destroy these rooms?" Sam asked.

"Guardians, actually," Tobias replied. "They destroyed and hid a lot of the Dreamer artifacts. But they were known by a different name then."

"So, like the Egyptian Guardians now?" Sam said. "Guardians who destroy what they were sworn to protect?"

"History is a complicated thing," Tobias said, nodding. "Things happen that years and decades and centuries later make little or no sense to us. But at the time, they were seen as a necessity."

"History is no less complicated than our future," Yutaka said, chuckling.

"What do you use this for, sir?" Issey asked.

"I come here sometimes," Yutaka said, "to meditate, to sleep on a problem, and I usually find what I need. It's not a place that will always tell you what you *want* to hear. But it seems to tell me what I need to know."

"Sam," Tobias said, looking at an imposing stone throne in the centre of the room, directly below the pinnacle of the crystal. "I think you should try too—to see if you can activate it. If that's alright, of course, Yutaka?"

The Prime Minister nodded.

"Activate it?" Sam said. He breathed in deeply and then

walked to the stone chair and sat down. The stone was not as cold and uninviting as he'd imagined it would be. It felt warm and contoured to his body.

The room was silent and Sam could feel the stares of the others. Waiting.

Sam closed his eyes and tried to relax.

The crystal above began to glow from within.

"What's happening?" Sam said. He looked around the room which was now lit up. The fine crystal that ran through the dark granite of the cavern walls glowed like a million fireflies were dancing around them.

"I've never seen it like this before . . ." Yutaka said, awestruck.

"It's like Sam is acting as a conductor," Tobias said. "He's completing the circuit."

Sam looked at the hairs on his arms—they were all standing up with the electricity in the room. Issey's hair too—his long black fringe, styled over one side of his face, was standing straight up in a fuzz.

"What's the room for, exactly?" Sam asked.

"We don't know," Tobias said. "No writing has been left behind to ever reveal its true purpose. But Dreamers think that spaces like this were made by ancient people to give them access to the Dreamscape."

"Wow . . ." Issey said. "To just watch dreams or to go into dreams and control them?"

"Very possibly both," Yutaka said.

"A manual would really come in handy, then," Sam joked.

"What do you feel?" Issey asked.

"Hungry," Sam replied, and the four of them laughed.

"When I come here, and sit in the seat," Yutaka said, "I get an immediate feeling of clarity. Answers to complex problems start to make sense to me. And I leave feeling energized—although the room does not light up like *this*."

"Where does this energy come from?" Sam asked.

"The earth," Tobias replied. "It's the oldest mode of energy—used by ancient civilizations. Have you heard of ley lines? Unseen lines criss-crossing the earth, deep in the land, that create natural currents. Lots of ancient stone structures, like Stonehenge in England, are said to be built on them or where they intersect."

"The Chinese called them Dragon Lines and gave the energy the name 'Chi,'" Yutaka added. "They buried kings and built palaces on these lines. Some historians believe the Egyptians learned a way to control this energy and use it."

"And I've never heard of them," Sam mused.

"Probably because you weren't paying enough attention in my classes—" Tobias laughed, but stopped suddenly as the chamber started to shake. It was only a distant rumble at first, flakes of dust floating down from the ceiling to land gently on their shoulders.

Sam eased out of the chair, alarmed by the confusion on Yutaka's face. Just then a deafening cracking sound thundered through the space, sending clouds of dust billowing up around them as they cried out.

ALEX

"I did do some work for Councillor Mac, it's true," Ahmed said to Alex, "but I never worked *for* him. In fact, as it turned out, being in his company was quite enlightening. Information I have since shared with many others."

Alex eyed the Egyptologist carefully. He stayed silent, thinking through what Ahmed had said. Challenging him further, accusing him of being a traitor, would probably mean Ahmed, and Hans, wouldn't share vital information with him.

Be cool, Alex. Find out what you can about whatever Hans is doing out here . . .

He let it go and tried to appear satisfied with Ahmed's explanation. He proceeded to reach over the table and load up a plate with food.

Hans sat down with a spread before him and began to pick at it. "So!" he said breaking the silence. "Here we all are, embarking on a great adventure together!"

Alex smiled awkwardly through his mouthful, not sure what to make of Hans' exuberance at their little lunch party and thinking about what an unlikely group they were for an "adventure."

"This ship," Ahmed said, looking up from the journal, "can she handle the ice?"

Alex was preoccupied with the journal, still desperate to know how Hans had stolen it from the Academy, but then his mind snapped taut with another thought.

Ice? What ice is there in the middle of the Pacific?

"Oh, yes," Hans was saying. "You'd better believe it my friend—the *Ra* has more than a few surprises in her yet!"

Ahmed laughed and turned to smile at Alex.

"You're Xavier's godfather, right?" Alex asked him, seizing the opportunity.

Ahmed nodded. "That's right."

"Did you always know?" Alex asked.

"Know what?"

"That he'd be one of the last 13," Alex said.

"Oh no, I had no idea," Ahmed said. "But I must say, I am very pleased. Destiny, it would seem."

Alex nodded as he sipped his drink. "And his father, Dr. Dark?" he added.

"I don't believe he had any idea either."

"What's he up to, then?" Alex persisted.

"Dr. Dark?"

"I haven't heard of him for a while," Alex said. "I saw him in Berlin. I haven't heard much about him since."

"I'm sure he's helping out wherever he can," Ahmed said.

"Perhaps you should ask your Academy sources though—Dr. Dark would be in touch with his son." A small smile played on the edges of Dr. Kader's mouth.

"Why don't you tell him, Ahmed," Hans said to the Egyptologist, "about why your good friend Dr. Dark sponsors all your research work? Tell Alex why he is so interested in the Dream Gate."

Dr. Kader looked from Hans to the stacks of notes before him, and then started to speak slowly, "Another time, maybe, I'm sure Alex here doesn't w—"

"Nonsense!" Hans interjected. "Now is a wonderful time. Alex would love to hear about Dr. Dark's views on what lies beyond the Dream Gate."

Dr. Kader sighed and spoke without looking up. "Dark has ideas—about the Dream Gate, and its potential powers. He . . . he's a specialist, of dreams, you see?"

"He's a psychiatrist," Alex said. "I know. So what? You're saying that he wants to help out the whole world with their dreams?"

"Some would say help," Hans said, chuckling. "Others might say control . . ."

Alex could see that Dr. Kader was uncomfortable with the conversation.

"Hans, please," Ahmed said, looking frustrated. "Dark is just like anyone else, he wants to know what lies beyond the Dream Gate—this is a great thing to be happening in our lifetime. Perhaps you assume he wants the power to himself, as this is closer to your way of looking at things."

Hans just laughed off the remark, even though Alex was pretty sure Dr. Kader did not intend it as a compliment.

"We'll see, my good friend," Hans said, still smiling. "We'll see."

SAM

"It's blocked," Yutaka said. "The whole tunnel has come down."

They were all frantically searching the blocked entrance, looking for some kind of way out.

"Was it an earthquake?" Sam asked.

"No, that was definitely the sound of explosives," Tobias said. "Yutaka, you must tell us, could there be anyone else who knows of this place?"

"Only the Japanese Guardians," Yutaka said. "I am certain. No one else . . ."

"What is it?" Sam asked, seeing the Japanese Prime Minister fall silent.

Tobias looked crestfallen. "The Guardians . . . ?"

Yutaka shook his head. "They were on the island with you last night."

"No, they weren't," Tobias said grimly.

"I sent them there, to save you," Yutaka said.

"We were alone, I'm afraid," Tobias said.

"I didn't see them on the island," Sam confirmed. "You think they did this?"

Tobias nodded.

"But I don't understand," Issey said. "I thought Yutaka just said they were meant to protect our leaders, to help Dreamers."

Tobias was silent. He was looking around the chamber with his flashlight. It was a useless search. The space, no bigger than half a basketball court, was closed tight.

Sam sat in the chair again, and, as before, the room was suddenly illuminated with the subtle light of a thousand stars.

Issey looks scared.

He's probably wondering about what it might be like to be trapped down here for the rest of his life.

Me too.

"Some of the Guardians," Sam said to Issey, steadying his voice, "have a different sense of purpose. They believe that they are here to protect the Dream Gate, to keep it secret. They don't protect Dreamers themselves. We had this problem before with the Egyptian Guardians."

That's not helping, is it?

There was a rumble from the entrance as more stone broke from the ceiling and settled into place.

"I was so proud of our Guardians," Yutaka said, anger flitting across his face, "so sure of their loyalty. I was blind to what was happening all around me. This is the one thing I imagined was impossible. My trust has been betrayed by the only ones who could have found us here."

"So, what you're saying is . . ." Issey trailed off.

"There's no one left to rescue us," Sam finished for him.

Yutaka looked to the others, sadness in his eyes. "No one else knows we are here. We are doomed. And it's all my fault. Forgive me, my friends."

EVA

"That's great!" Eva said, sighing in relief. "Sam's OK?"

"Yes," the Professor replied. "He's under observation in hospital. Another close call, but he will be fine."

There was silence in the room for a while, with just the faint sounds of the students playing sports out on the fields of the London campus to break the lull.

"So, what does this attack mean for us?" Eva asked. "For the competition?"

"The Four Corners Competition will continue as planned," the Professor said. "I have spoken with the other teams and with the Dreamer Council, and everyone agrees that it is necessary to proceed. The judging delegation will be arriving at the tournament tomorrow. It will go ahead."

"But we need four teams, don't we?" Xavier asked.

Eva looked at Zara and Xavier, who had been quietly listening to the discussion.

They look worried and scared. Will we be OK in the competition? How can we do what we need to with all this going on around us?

"No," Lora replied. "Usually, the competition is made up

of teams of three students from each of the four Academies. But it is not a condition of the competition—it has gone ahead with three teams, or teams with fewer participants."

"So we will still leave this afternoon?" Zara said.

"Yes," Lora replied. "I'll be accompanying you as planned."

"Remember," the Professor said, "This year's competition is different from any that has come before."

"Yes, Professor," Xavier said, "we know. We will be using the competition and our time in the dream construct to find the missing Gears."

"To locate where Solaris has put them," Zara said, almost at the same time.

"That's right," the Professor said.

"What if the other teams win too quickly and it is all over before we can find the Gears?" Eva asked. "The 2007 competition was won inside of six hours."

Lora smiled, said, "That was me and Seb, and another student, Prue."

"How'd you get the prize so quickly?" Zara asked.

"I think we were lucky," Lora said.

"And the three of you were very skilled," the Professor said. "It was the most spectacular tournament in more than a hundred years. You should all watch the recording before you leave, it might give you some useful pointers." He smiled at Lora.

"So you can record them like regular dreams? Like the one you showed me before?" Eva asked.

"Yes, and no," the Professor said. "Because the competition is held in a dream *construct*, rather than the real Dreamscape. It is created in the previous winner's mind and cannot be manipulated except by them. Only the official judges monitoring it can record the events within."

"Huh," Xavier said. "You'd think something artificially constructed would be easier to manipulate than the actual Dreamscape."

"You make it sound like you are going into a computer game, but it's not," the Professor said. "The Doors construct feels as real as any dream you've had, but it is on another dreamwave, one that is not accessed by your sleeping mind. But it's far closer to the dark part of your mind that controls nightmares than you'd like to think."

"And who's running it?" Xavier asked. "Who sets up the doors and hides the prize inside the construct?"

"The doors were placed there a long, long time ago," the Professor said. "And believe me, it is not as bad now as it was during the Dark Ages. The prizes, well, they are placed there by the governing delegates."

"You will only truly understand it once you enter the construct," Lora said. "It's just everything is a little . . . strange—unpredictable."

"And your minds will instinctively bring into the space what you fear most," the Professor said. "There is no avoiding that."

SAM

Sam stopped digging and caught his breath. The smaller pieces of stone they had moved easily, the larger rocks had been pushed aside with their combined effort. Two hours' work and they'd gotten little closer to salvation, and now the four stood silent, utterly spent of energy. Sam leaned against the wall.

"It's impossible," Issey said. He went to sit on a boulder the size of a refrigerator.

Sam looked at the contents of their pockets spread out on the stone floor.

Wallets, phones that had no reception, a couple of flashlights, a pocket knife, a notebook and Tobias' dart gun.

"What do we do?" Issey asked. "What *can* we do?"

"I think I need to do what I do best," Sam said, heading for the chair in the middle of the chamber. "Sleep."

"Of course!" Tobias said, wrapping bits of his torn suit jacket around the scratches covering his hands. "That's it!"

Sam sank into the chair, every muscle aching. Once again, the crystals lit up the room.

"Sam," Tobias said, "It's possible that the chair will

give you the same clarity of thought as it does for Yutaka, perhaps even more. Your dreams are the best hope we have of finding a way out."

"OK," Sam said, closing his eyes. "That's sort of what I was thinking too." And then he added in a tired, drawn-out voice, "Dream of a phone, call Lora for help. Or Superman, he would do . . ."

Issey laughed, which, despite their circumstances, made Sam feel better. He had been growing more concerned about the Japanese Dreamer, who looked like the events of the last twenty-four hours were bringing him closer and closer to breaking down in despair. Sam had been the last to keep digging, to try to give him even the smallest amount of hope.

"Sam, you need to steer your dream," Tobias said, pacing back and forth in front of the stone chair. "Dream of us getting out of here."

With his eyes still closed, Sam gave a thumbs up, again trying to lighten the mood in the room. The others were silent, Sam could tell by their slight movements that they stayed where they were—sitting on the floor and leaning against the walls, waiting.

"Think he's sleeping?" Issey whispered after a moment.

"No," Sam said, smiling, but keeping his eyes closed. "He's not. Geez, give me a bit of time. I'd wait for the snoring to start at least . . ."

It took Sam nearly an hour to fall asleep. When he

dreamed, it was of a man he'd last seen locked in battle with Solaris.

"Did you hear that?" Issey said, rushing to the caved-in entrance and listening. "Someone's out there! And it sounds like they have heavy machinery!"

Sam heard it. In fact, it was the noise that had startled him awake only a few seconds before—it rumbled like distant thunder.

"That's not just machines," Tobias said. "Someone's blasting through!"

"That'll be our help," Sam said, remaining seated in the stone chair so that the room was illuminated by the glow of the crystals.

"Sam!" Issey said, turning around. "You've been asleep for hours!"

"Two, according to my watch," Sam replied, then rubbed the sleep from his face and stretched out. A massive granite chair, Sam now knew, was no relaxing recliner in which to snooze, no matter how well-crafted and worn with age it might be.

"Did you dream?" Tobias asked. His eyes were wide with expectation, like he had already figured out the answer.

"It was really weird. I dreamed I was talking to someone. Nothing else happened, we just talked."

"Could that friend be here already?" Yutaka asked.

Another blast echoed through the chamber.

"Um, yes," Sam said, starting to smile. "I'd say so."

It took another twenty minutes for daylight to spill through the cave-in at the chamber entrance. A lone figure was standing there, looking squat and steadfast in stance. They could make out the profile behind him of a digger—some kind of bulldozer.

The man was shadowed and unidentifiable in the glare of the bright light behind, as everyone's eyes struggled to adjust to the light.

Sam, though, knew instantly who it was. He'd spoken to him in his dream, explained where they were and asked him for help.

It was Issey who realized first.

"*Ojiisan!*"

Issey ran to his grandfather and hugged him tight.

"I thought—I thought . . ." Issey couldn't bring himself to say what they all had been thinking.

We thought you were dead, killed protecting us from Solaris.

"Dead?" Kaga said, his face breaking into a big smile. "It takes more than a fire-breathing *oni* to destroy Kaga."

11

ALEX

Alex fiddled with his food as Ahmed carefully turned the pages of da Vinci's journal. The paper was heavy, each page full of notes and diagrams. From across the table Alex could see the writing was barely legible, an excited scrawl written in another language. The pictures and illustrations, however, were extraordinary.

"What's that?" Alex asked, pointing to a sketch.

"That's what everyone is searching for," Hans said.

"Yes," Ahmed said, staring at it.

"Really?" Alex said. He stood and walked over to stand next to Ahmed and looked down at the drawing.

It's the Bakhu Machine but with the Gears pieced together within it. I never did get to see the journal while it was at the Academy. Finally I'm getting a look at what all this has been for.

"It's incredible . . ."

Alex was back in his cabin on the *Ra*. Like the main dining room, it looked like an expensive hotel suite, complete with all the amenities he could want. There was a phone too, a cordless handset. He tried it for reception and was surprised to get a dial tone.

Must be satellite.

He sat on the edge of the bed for a while and stared at it.

I should call my mother. Tell her where I am. Get them to track the boat.

Alex picked up the phone and started to dial and then put it back into the cradle.

What if Hans and his guys are listening in on the phones as well?

Alex glanced around his small room.

I should have a poke around, see if there's another way to make contact.

Alex left his room on a scouting expedition. He moved quietly, his bare feet silent on the carpet. He walked down the hall off the living quarters to a small lounge area at the bow of the *Ra*. He didn't pass anyone, not the boat's crew or any of the security guys he recognized as being rogue German Guardians.

Where is everyone?

The floor under his feet hummed with the constant vibration of the boat's engines.

Still running at full steam.

He looked out a porthole window. From the position of the sun, he knew that they were still headed south in the Pacific Ocean, on a boat decked out for an icy voyage.

Could be headed for somewhere on the southern coast of South America, or . . . where? Maybe east, toward Asia? Or south-east to Australia and New Zealand? We could be headed anywhere. Or nowhere . . . maybe this is just another form of kidnapping?

Alex shook off his rambling thoughts and went into a small conference room off to the side of the lounge area, closing the door carefully behind him. He was still on the same level as the sleeping quarters, the deck below the level where he'd had lunch a few hours before. The conference room was roughly the size of his own room but was furnished with a long table and ten chairs. The walls were covered in digital screens and telecommunications gear. On a bench that ran along the end wall, several satellite phones sat in a row.

This must be the nerve centre of the boat—the command and control room. If they were going to listen in to phone calls, this is where they'd do it. Maybe I could re-wire a phone, or check it for listening bugs . . . where's Shiva when I need him?

Alex looked at one of the phones, picking up the cordless handset and inspecting it carefully, before also scrutinizing the docking cradle.

Should I? It doesn't look like it's plugged into a listening device.

He picked up the handset and dialed his mother's number. She answered on the second ring.

"This is Phoebe."

"Mom—" Alex said in a whisper.

"Alex! Where are you?" Her voice was urgent and frightened. "When we saw those men come in, I didn't know what to think!"

"Mom, it's OK, I'm fine. I'm at sea—"

"At sea! With who?"

"Hans. But it's OK."

"Hans!" Phoebe's voice went up an octave as she spoke.

"Shh. Relax, OK? I'm fine. Wait one sec."

Alex pressed a button on a remote, flicking a nearby screen to life. The weather channel played loudly over speakers, hopefully drowning out any eavesdroppers to Alex's side of the conversation.

"What's that noise?"

"It's just a precaution. I turned the TV on so people can't hear what I'm saying."

Phoebe was silent for a moment, then she said, "Shiva didn't know who had taken you. It happened so fast, he didn't have time to see anything. But *Hans* . . ."

"Hans is . . . look, it's all OK, Mom," Alex interrupted. "Is Shiva alright? What happened to Matrix?"

"Shiva's fine. He took a bump to the back of his head and a bit of a blow to his pride, but he's fine. Matrix is being held at the security wing of the Enterprise. Jack is there now, interrogating him, but he's not being very co-operative. Alex, are you saying that you went with Hans . . . willingly?"

"Um, sorta . . . yeah."

"Alex! Hans is *dangerous!*" Phoebe said, raising her voice again.

"Mom, calm down," Alex said. "We're on his ship, about five hours from Hawaii, I think, headed south at full steam."

"I'll come with a team to get you back."

"What? No, Mom, please. Listen," Alex said. "He trusts me, OK? Hans trusts me. He *asked* me to come along and I agreed. I'm not a prisoner."

"It may have looked like that, Alex, but he's used to getting what he wants."

"I know, Mom, I get that," Alex said. "Look, he's headed somewhere—somewhere I'm sure is important to the race to the Dream Gate. He has da Vinci's journal." The other end of the line was silent for a long time. "Mom . . . ?"

"How did . . . the Professor had informed me that it was stolen, but I didn't realize . . ." Phoebe said finally. "You're playing a dangerous game, Alex. Are you sure you know what you're doing?"

"Look, Mom, I'm safe for now. And I'm of use here—I can see what Hans is doing. I can report back to you. Be a spy. Just like Stella was doing, remember? You were watching her, to track her movements, right? I can do the same here. I can play along and see what Hans is up to."

"It's too dangerous."

"Danger is my middle name," Alex laughed.

"Your middle name is Stacy."

"Yeah, don't remind me, I got enough grief about that in school."

It was Phoebe's turn to laugh.

"Look, Mom, you said it yourself, Hans believes I'm valuable, so nothing will happen to me, right? So long as he's convinced that I'm one of the last 13, he's not gonna hurt me."

There was more silence. "OK, Alex," Phoebe said wearily, "I'll discuss this with the Director. But you be careful."

"Careful is my *new* middle name."

"But I want you to call in every day, about this time. OK? That way we can accurately keep track of you through the calls."

"OK," Alex said. "You got it."

Alex could hear his mother exhale, perhaps with relief, but probably with a sense of unease.

"Gee, Mom, worry much?"

"These people are dangerous," she repeated. "They're killers."

"But not like Solaris, not like Stella. This Hans guy is different. You'll see." Alex stopped when he thought he heard the soft thudding of approaching footsteps in the hallway outside. "Gotta go."

"OK," Phoebe said, before quickly adding, "call me tomorrow!"

Alex hung up the phone. He hurriedly picked up the screen remote, at the same time swinging both his feet up to rest on the bench in front of him.

The door to the room opened slowly.

Hans.

He looked at Alex, one eyebrow raised in suspicion.

"Hi!" Alex said casually.

Hans smiled. "Interested in the weather, I see," he said.

"Sure," Alex shrugged, and turned down the volume of the weather channel. "Actually, I was just snooping around, trying to find a games console. It's pretty boring at sea, you know."

"No time for games, Alex," Hans said, his smile widening. "Not yet. Come, I have a more productive way for you to spend this time."

12

SAM

"So the last you saw of Solaris," Sam said to Kaga, "was when he left you for dead in your house?"

"Yes," Kaga said, after recounting the full events of the night before as he drove them all in his car to a government airfield. "A ceiling beam had pinned me down. My fire-suit saved me, I was not harmed as I lay there, but I had to wait until the fire had burned through the wood beam for me to get out from under it. The brave firefighters came but they could not reach me."

"And Solaris?" Sam asked.

"When he saw that I was trapped, and that the flames would consume the house, he disappeared. Like the coward he is."

"And we know the rest," Tobias said. "He tracked us to Ghost Island, stole the Gear and destroyed our boat."

Or Stella has it. Either way . . .

"But how did you dream of Grandfather?" Issey asked Sam in wonder.

"I'm not sure," Sam said, watching the Tokyo skyline flash by out the window. "I just relaxed as much as I could and I kept thinking about what Yutaka said, about letting the answers come to you. Then the memory of Kaga fighting Solaris, that unforgettable image, was the next thing I saw."

"It's a good thing," Tobias said. "And not just because you were able to get Kaga, who was so close by, to come and save us. It also proves what a powerful Dreamer you are, Sam. By letting your mind take you where it needed to go, you saved us all. With practice, with time, you will be able to achieve great things."

"But that's just it, isn't it?" Sam said. "If only we *had* time. If only I could practise, right? We don't even know how long we have left to finish this race and I'm only just starting to be able to use my dreams to *do* something. If I ever work out how to become a Dreamer like you and Lora and the Professor, it might be too late."

"No," Tobias said. "You're not like us. Your abilities are far beyond us all. And you must believe this race will not be the end of things. It will be a truly amazing beginning."

The Japanese Prime Minister nodded along as Tobias spoke.

"It will?" Issey said.

"He means," Sam said, "it's not the end—so long as we win. So long as *we're* the ones to get all the Gears and use the Bakhu machine to find the Dream Gate."

"Yes," Tobias said. "That's about the size of it."

Kaga drove his old Toyota toward the gates of an airfield. Several soldiers, in full uniform and holding weapons, approached as they slowed to a stop in front of the checkpoint.

"Wait a moment in the car, please," Yutaka said. He climbed out of the passenger seat and confidently headed toward the men.

I guess he's their ultimate boss.

As the Prime Minister walked closer, Sam watched the recognition register on the faces of the base guards, who smartly, and as one, stood to attention and snapped off salutes. The gate was opened immediately and Yutaka returned to the car after a short conversation with the guards. Kaga drove on, this time following a military vehicle that guided them to a long row of hangars.

"You will be flown wherever you need to go," Yutaka said to Sam. "The pilots will take your orders and fly to any destination in the world."

"Wow . . ." Issey said.

"Thank you," Tobias said, bowing his head to Yutaka, "you are very kind." Then he turned to the others in the car. "Kaga, can you escort Issey to the Academy in London?"

"Of course," Kaga said.

"Sam and I have a new Dreamer to meet," Tobias said.

"What about Solaris and the Gear that he took from us?" Issey said. "Or do you think the woman has it now?"

Sam and Tobias said nothing. Eventually Tobias answered, "One step at a time I think, Issey. And that will no doubt be our next challenge."

The car drove into a large hangar filled with several gleaming white passenger jets. Some were small aircraft that looked to only be four- or six-seaters, others were larger, official-looking jets that would carry more than twenty passengers.

"So maybe he's added one more to his collection," Sam said, almost as if thinking out loud. "So what? We're going to have to get all the Gears he has anyway. What does it matter if it's two, or three or four?"

The car came to a stop and they got out. Kaga handed the keys to a base soldier.

"So that's the next step—we just hunt him down?" Issey said. "Battle him until he gives up his Gears?"

"Issey, there will be no need to hunt Solaris," Kaga said to his grandson. "*He* will come for Sam." Then he turned and put a hand on Sam's shoulder, speaking quietly. "Remember, don't be afraid. Look at me, I'm old, and I survived."

Sam nodded, and said his goodbyes to Issey and Kaga. Kaga shook Tobias' hand and bowed to the Japanese Prime Minister before walking up the narrow stairs into the cabin of one of the small planes, closely followed by Issey and four armed guards.

"Good luck, Sam," Yutaka said, shaking Sam's hand. "It has been an honour to spend time with you, however difficult the circumstances."

Sam smiled, said, "Likewise, Mr. Prime Minister. Thank

you for looking after us. And for arranging all this for us."

"The least I could do," Yutaka said. "And I mean that with all sincerity. And I promise you that when we next talk, it will be in New York, where I will arrange that audience for you, and we can bring the whole world to this fight."

"We look forward to it," Tobias said. "Thank you."

"In the meantime," Yutaka said, looking to his armed soldiers, standing at attention to one side. "I will find the Guardians who trapped us in the Yume Uchū. They will not be given the chance to harm another Dreamer, you have my word."

"Thank you again," Sam said. He walked with Tobias to board the jet, bound for their next destination and the next Dreamer, Poh.

13

ALEX

"I still don't know where we're going," Alex whispered into the phone to his mother.

It was late and he was curled up on one of the chairs in the control room once more, the satellite phone handset wedged between his ear and his shoulder. His hand rested on the TV remote control, ready, in case he needed to make it look like he was in there watching the big screen again.

"What's wrong?" Phoebe asked, alarmed. "You sound different. Is everything OK?"

"Yeah, yeah. Just tired."

"Get out at the next port. Leave Hans, it doesn't matter. We can monitor his movements remotely."

"No, Mom, I'll stay. It's better this way," Alex said. "From what I can tell, we're headed to Australia. A place called Cairns is our next stop. I checked the ship's itinerary when no one was around. We're supposed to be there late tomorrow night. Then, from there to Christchurch for a refuel and resupply. After that, the itinerary is blank."

"I don't like the sound of that, Alex. Get off in Australia—we'll pick you up from there."

"But that's the whole point—that's the reason I have to stay," Alex said, still weary, "to find out. Dr. Kader asked Hans if this ship can handle ice. That's not just a random question, is it? Hans is obviously going south, *far* south, to somewhere he doesn't want even his captain to know about."

"I don't like this," his mother said again. "We have satellite tracking on the *Ra* now, Alex, we can follow where Hans is going from here at the Enterprise. You've done enough."

"Mom, you know how unreliable that can be," Alex said. "We lose satellite connections all the time. Or they can be hacked into. You know this better than I do, right? It's always better to stay in the field. If I'm here, I can try to find out where we're going before we get there. And if I talk to Ahmed, maybe even get him on his own, I could find out why we are going there. Wouldn't it be better to know what Hans is looking for . . . or hiding?"

"Hans has already shown how unstable and reckless he can be. And this is all just speculation. It could be a big waste of time," Phoebe said. "Or an attempt to get you out of the way . . ."

"Look, Mom, I promise, if it starts to look dicey, I'll get out at the next port and get on the first plane home."

"Alex . . ." There was a long pause on the other end of the line. "Fine, OK."

"OK?" Alex smiled. "Really? Finally! Thanks, Mom. Can you do one thing for me, though?"

"Of course, anything," Phoebe said quickly. "What do you need?"

"Next time I call, can we just skip past the part where you tell me I have to come back immediately and I have to convince you that I'm OK over and over?"

Phoebe laughed. "Hmm, we'll see. There is something you can do for me too—the day after tomorrow, tune into the international news channel at 5pm Eastern Time, US."

"Why?"

"There is a special broadcast scheduled, from inside the UN General Assembly."

"That sounds boring," Alex said. "What's happening there?"

"Just tune in. You *won't* find it boring, I promise."

"Alright, Mom. Talk to you soon."

"*Tomorrow*," Phoebe corrected. "And Alex?"

"Yeah?"

"I love you. Be careful."

"Yeah, thanks, Mom. Back at ya."

14

SAM

Sam's first impression of Cambodia was that it was a friendly place. The faces of the people he saw were happy and welcoming and there was a kindness in the people he spoke to. His next impression was of the weather. It carried a tropical heat and stickiness, and then the noise—thousands of motorbikes and scooters, buses and vans, all tooting horns and ringing bells.

Sam *loved* it.

The flight there on the Japanese plane had been quick and easy, and Sam and Tobias both had managed to rest. And now, here they were, headed once more to the next Dreamer. The odds felt better this time around—they were already in the country, they were alone and not being followed by anyone they knew of. There was an unspoken positive mood between them.

Or maybe it's just that we've both recently been miraculously rescued from a slow death trapped underground. That'd put a spring in anyone's step. Ha!

Tobias walked out of the hotel foyer where he'd gone to ask for directions from the concierge. He weaved through the traffic across the road to Sam, who was sitting in a small park under the shade of a coconut tree.

"I don't think you're supposed to sit under coconut trees," Tobias said. "More people are killed by falling coconuts than in shark attacks, you know."

"Really? Where'd you get that statistic? The Internet?" Sam scoffed, but he couldn't help looking up the tall trunk to where he could see four large coconuts. "I think, in the scheme of things, this is the *least* dangerous thing I've done in a while. Besides, I also recall from some lame class back at school," he said, pushing himself up off the grass, "that something like two thousand people per year die as a direct result of using a right-handed instrument, like a power saw."

"Ah, yes. Another fascinating lesson of mine. And it was two thousand five hundred *left-handed* people," Tobias corrected. "Which is half as many as those who die each year falling out of bed."

"Is that so?" Sam laughed. "But it does all make sense now—you taught that class as a warning to me, because I'm a Dreamer and so I'm often asleep, usually in a bed, and I'm left-handed. And here we are, under a coconut tree, having only been nearly eaten by a shark last week."

"Exactly," Tobias said. "So you would agree that I am a master teacher after all?"

"Sure. Or . . . *or*, maybe I'm indestructible," Sam joked. "Let's just say the jury is still out and we'd both better be wary of dodgy facts."

"Fair call," Tobias said. "What do you say about getting back to this saving the world business then?"

"Right, I'm ready," Sam said, stretching out his back. "Just point me in the right direction and consider it done. No problem."

Tobias laughed. "We have a couple of options to get to Angkor Wat, where you dreamed of Poh. We can catch a bus or a boat out of the city to Siem Reap."

"That's where Angkor is?" Sam asked. "How long's the journey?"

"About five hours, either option."

Sam thought about it. "Boat."

"Good choice," Tobias said. "We should be safer on the water."

15

EVA

Eva woke from a disturbed sleep.

I'm still in London.

Outside it was a grey afternoon. She'd hardly slept through the night, worried about Sam, and the nap she'd just taken felt as though it had done little to replenish her strength.

"Sleep on the plane," she said to herself, packing her bag. "Sleep for the competition. Dream later."

She paused and looked at the photo of her surrogate parents on her bedside table, and then, as an afterthought, she packed that in the bag too. She zipped up the backpack, slung it over her shoulder and left her room, meeting Zara and Xavier at the landing at the top of the stairs.

"Ready?" she asked them.

"Yes," Xavier said. "I can't wait. This is going to be awesome!"

"Careful what you wish for," Eva said, forcing a smile and trying to sound like she was joking. A strong surge of guilt washed over her as a recurring thought jumped back into her head—*I wish it were Alex and Sam coming with me.*

On the flight to Istanbul, where the Dreamer Doors was to be held, Eva sat in between Xavier and Zara in the centre aisle of the plane. Lora and two Guardians sat four rows ahead of them, with more Guardians dispersed throughout the plane.

They compared notes about their dreams and nightmares, and mused over what they could expect to find once inside the competition construct. Eva noticed that the lady across the aisle from Xavier looked his way a few times, apparently offended by the frightening details he was describing from his worst imaginable nightmare. Eva nudged Xavier with her elbow.

"Ow! Hey! What was that for?" Xavier asked her. Eva tilted her head in the direction of the frowning lady.

Xavier turned to face the woman. He flashed his trademark smile and leaned over, holding out his packet of snacks across the aisle. "So sorry to disturb you, ma'am," he said smoothly. "We'll keep it down. Pretzel?"

Her expression softened and she smiled as she declined his offer. Eva rolled her eyes.

"Now," Xavier said, resuming their conversation, "remember what Lora told us, if we dare to face our nightmare, we might come out of it better off."

"Yeah, it's the 'might' bit that worries me," Eva said.

"We have to find a way to stay in the construct as long

as we can," said Zara, "or we'll never find where Solaris has hidden our Gears."

Eva nodded, thinking. "Maybe there's a loophole here. I mean, if we have to face our worst nightmare, does it specify from *when*? What if, instead of my worst nightmare *now*—

"A bad hair day?" Xavier joked.

Eva punched him in the leg. "No, but instead of that," she said, "maybe I could try and steer it to be my worst nightmare from when I was like ten, or five."

"What was that?" Xavier said. "A unicorn dying? Your favourite boy band breaking up?"

"I think you are talking about *your* nightmares," Zara said, and the girls cracked up laughing.

"Seriously though, do you think that could work?" Eva said. "My nightmare then was that I'd climbed to the top of the highest tree in our backyard and I couldn't get down."

"Gee, that sounds scary," Xavier said.

"Do you not see what Eva is saying?" Zara said. "We could try to conjure the nightmare to be something that we can more easily deal with now, right, Eva?"

"Right," Eva replied. "Though I still don't like heights. How about you guys?"

"I was scared of the dark," Zara said. "Still now, a little, though I can better control it, my fear I mean."

"OK," Eva said. "Xavier?"

He was looking away from them, absently staring up

the aisle toward the front of the big commercial aircraft.

"Xav?" Eva said after he'd been silent for a minute.

"My father," Xavier said, still looking away.

"Dr. Dark?" Eva asked, shocked.

"I don't mean I'm afraid *of* him. He . . . my mother, she . . . I was very young when I lost her, and I remember being terrified that I would lose my dad, too."

Zara made a note in her notebook.

She loves writing stuff down . . . that could come in handy.

"I guess that it would still be my greatest fear now, though," Xavier added. "That's not going to help much with your theory, is it?"

"I think we'll be fine," Eva said to her teammates, "*all* of us. So long as we try to be smart about this, and do our best not to bring our scariest thoughts into the construct. No terrifying zombie unicorns with bad hair singing in a boy band in *this* dream world, right?"

Xavier burst into loud laughter, and then quickly had to apologize to the passenger across the aisle again. Eva and Zara giggled. The three of them continued their plotting and planning for the competition ahead.

Now we're starting to feel like a team.

16

SAM

The boat took them out onto the Mekong River, and journeyed north to where the river forked into two. They veered slightly to the north-west, ambling along the Tonlé Sap river, which eventually opened up to an expansive lake. There was endless water as far as Sam could see in either direction. Boats were coming and going, trading seafood and agricultural produce to locals and tourists along the river banks.

Sam and Tobias sat on the roof of the boat. The afternoon sun was baking hot, but the slight breeze in the open air made it much more bearable than sitting in the crowded, stifling confines below.

"Tobias?"

"Yep?" Tobias watched Sam, waiting patiently.

"In my dreams," Sam said, staring at the water in the lake as the boat cut through it, "I mean, not always but since this began . . ."

"Yes? What about them?"

"They are . . . I mean, sometimes I dream of a different time and different place to where I am." Sam watched the watercraft move by, most of them faster than their ferry. It felt as though they were heading in the right direction but going too slow.

Just like I feel in this race—as though we're never quite moving fast enough to beat the others to the finish line.

"Where are these dreams set?" Tobias asked.

"Egypt. It's always Egypt," Sam said. "That much doesn't change. The time is what changes. By ages—years, decades, centuries. Sometimes I'm there when they're building the pyramids. Once I saw them carving the Sphinx. Other times I'm an explorer, or a soldier. Either way, I'm always passing through and seeing things as though for the first time, but somehow I know what they are and where I am."

"What else do you remember?"

"I remember some things clearly, as though they really happened. Yesterday I dreamed I was with Roman legionnaires. It was way back, like maybe in the first centuries. The day before I was with Napoleon's troops in the nineteenth century."

"Why have you never talked about these dreams before?" Tobias asked gently.

"Well, I know the Professor has been watching my dreams and he never mentioned them. So I just ignored them."

"And now?" Tobias urged.

"They're cramming in more and more. It's harder to ignore them. And now I'm wondering what they might really mean." Sam sighed and ran his fingers through his dusty hair.

"You should trust your dreams," Tobias said. "Follow them. If they show you Egypt, then you should learn all about who reigned when, who built the pyramids, and why."

"Is all that written down somewhere?"

"A million and one places," Tobias laughed.

"Even the reasons why?"

"Well . . ."

"Besides, I thought the age was debated. Many people believe the Sphinx was made thousands of years earlier than everything else on the Giza plateau, right?"

Tobias smiled. "Trust yourself. Let your dreams help you."

"What do *you* think it all means?"

Tobias sighed. "Perhaps the Dream Gate is somewhere in Egypt."

"Really?" Sam turned to face him eagerly.

"The Dream Stele, the Star of Egypt—all began with Ramses. The Ancient Egyptians knew about it. They probably used it. It wouldn't surprise me if it was hidden there."

"Do you have evidence of that?"

Tobias shrugged and sipped from his water bottle. "Don't have any evidence to the contrary," he said.

They were silent for a while, watching the water and the other boats cruising by.

"Makes you wonder, though," Tobias said. "The things that the Egyptians did, what they made, the marvel of it all—the pyramids, all of it, was incredible."

"*Too* incredible?" Sam asked.

"Are you realizing that we'd have a tough time building the pyramids with today's knowledge and technology, let alone construct something so advanced?"

"Advanced?"

"What they were really made for," Tobias added. He chuckled. "Maybe I've been listening to the Professor too long."

"But what about what happens when we find the Gate?" Sam said. "I mean, we *have* to open it, right?"

"Yes, I think we have to. If we don't, someone else will," Tobias said.

"Unless . . ."

"Sam?"

"Unless we hide it again. Make it tougher to find," Sam said.

Tobias laughed. "What, this isn't tough enough?"

"Yeah, you're right," Sam said as he flicked the flies away from his face. "But I just worry that if the power that lies beyond the Gate is so great, maybe it *shouldn't* be opened. Maybe we're not ready for it yet. Maybe it *should* be destroyed."

Tobias turned sharply to look at Sam, but said nothing.

17

ALEX

"Where are we headed?" Alex asked as he and Hans headed down a sprawling metal spiral staircase.

"To Ahmed's workroom," Hans replied.

"No," Alex said, "I mean all of us, on this ship."

"I like to think of it more as a superyacht," Hans said. "Or, more specifically, the *Ra*."

"Named after the ancient Egyptian sun god?"

"Yes."

"OK, Hans, tell me—where's the *Ra* headed?"

"South," Hans replied. "We are headed south."

"Right. Well, I figured that much out by looking through the window." The two of them paused at the landing at the bottom of the stairs. This level was dark, the floor covered with black rubber decking.

The ship's workrooms, probably the kitchens and staff quarters.

"The direction of the sun, the time of day, we're headed south," Alex repeated.

"You figured that out because you're smart," Hans said, "And yes, you are correct. We are headed south—*far* south."

Alex nodded, understanding now something that Ahmed had asked about earlier. "That's why Ahmed asked if this ship—ahem, the *Ra*—could handle navigating through ice. What's all that way down there that we need?"

Hans stopped and smiled at Alex. "Everything," he said. "Everything we need is down there."

Everything we need? Like what? The machine? His secret lair? Are there other people in the race down there?

Alex couldn't shake the stark fact that he'd have to wait a while to find out. And he didn't like waiting. He stood his ground. "*Tell* me," he said to Hans.

Hans stared at him as though he was weighing up the pros and cons of doing so.

"You want me to tag along and help you on your little adventure? Then I gotta know," Alex said. "Don't make me swim back to shore in protest."

But Hans just laughed and pushed open a heavy door and waved him inside. "Enjoy! I'll see you later."

As Alex stepped in, he could see Ahmed's workroom was set up like an ancient library, full of scrolls and books, but with a modern-day computer lab twist. All kinds of high-tech gear lay scattered about the room.

"Come in, come in!" Ahmed exclaimed. He took Alex's arm and steered him toward a large screen. Scanned images from da Vinci's journal were projected onto it.

"What's that?" Alex asked, his nose up against the huge monitor that showed an unfamiliar sketch.

"This is a drawing of the Schist Disc. The actual disc is now housed at the Cairo museum," Ahmed said. "It was found in Saqqara, in a burial tomb that to this day no one is allowed to visit."

"Why can't anyone visit it?"

"Because they may find more objects that cannot be explained."

Alex shrugged. "When was this disc found?"

"A long time after da Vinci sketched this illustration in his journal."

"So what does that mean? That the disc had not yet been lost or buried in da Vinci's time?"

"No. That disc was found at a datable layer of excavation, many centuries before da Vinci's time in the 1500s."

"So there's another one of these discs—one that da Vinci saw."

"That is the most likely explanation," Ahmed agreed.

"What was it used for?" Alex asked.

"What do you think it looks like?" Ahmed countered.

"A steering wheel? Or the wheel for a machine of some sort. Maybe the top of a huge tap?"

"Yes, it could be any of those things. We do not yet know for sure, that is the mystery," Ahmed said.

"Amazing . . ." Alex looked to him. "Sam mentioned you."

"Oh?"

"That he met you in Egypt, when you were working for Dr. Dark."

"Yes."

"Now you work for Hans?"

"Well, no, and to be technically correct, I've never really worked for anyone other than myself," Ahmed said. "Over the years many people have generously sponsored my expeditions and my research."

"So you're what? A scientist for hire?" Alex couldn't stop himself from scoffing.

"I am a *discoverer*, and like those in the sixteenth century who set out to find lost places and history, I need money to fund such expeditions."

"Sure," Alex said to appease him.

"These pages mention the device," Ahmed said, changing images so that what Alex was looking at was shown in larger format on the screen, "which as we know is translated as Bakhu machine but in actual fact is a mechanical map."

Alex nodded and walked around the room. He found a note in Egyptian hieroglyphics on parchment.

"What's this say?" he asked.

"That is a food order, a menu, from Ramses the Great."

"Wow. What'd he eat?"

Ahmed chuckled. "Not as much as we eat today."

"And this—what's this?" Alex held up a gold pendant.

"Ah, that," Ahmed said, and he leaned back on his stool, away from his workbench where he was studying his notes. "Egyptians had no word for death. Only 'westing,' as in the sun setting. *That* is an amulet they believed provided access to that world beyond."

"Wow . . ." Alex put it down, continuing his saunter around the room, looking over sketches and notes and maps. "Hans said something to me before, about power— power in the ground and that the pyramids are generators or conduits or something."

"Perhaps," Ahmed said. "Even I do not profess to know all the answers to the mysteries of the ancients. What I do know might not be of interest to you . . ."

"Try me," Alex insisted.

But their conversation was abruptly cut short when an alarm began to shriek, reverberating around the entire ship.

18

SAM

Sam decided that the dockside at Siem Reap was one of the most chaotic places he had ever seen.

"This makes dinnertime at the Academy look like a picnic," Sam joked to Tobias as they disembarked. The gangplank led them to a seething mass of humanity where they were surrounded immediately.

"Just stay close," Tobias replied, trying to stick next to Sam in the crowd of thousands of tourists and locals crammed tight.

There were soldiers too, Sam saw. Lots of them, in trucks and milling about at the far edges of the docks and market.

"Think that's a usual sight?" Sam asked.

"No," Tobias said. "It's because of the nightmares everyone's having. There's been plenty of trouble here, just like every other place around the world. Be careful."

At the side of the river, hawkers for lodgings, porters and tuktuk drivers competed noisily for customers. In among them all, dozens of street children swarmed everywhere. They pushed in between Sam and Tobias, all with dirty faces and outstretched searching hands.

Sam gave what few dollars he had left in his wallet to the kids around him, creating an even more furious frenzy, and followed Tobias to a clear spot in the road, many of the kids still following them, begging with big smiles.

"What do we do?" Sam asked.

"We find someone to drive us to Angkor Wat."

"I mean about them," Sam said, gesturing to those gathered behind him.

"Right now, nothing," Tobias said. "Sorry, I know it's hard. But the race is for the good of everyone and we have to keep our focus on that. This way."

Tobias weaved through a crowd of tourists buying trinkets from stalls, and they came to a row of tuktuks with drivers standing by them. Sam looked back and the sight broke his heart.

"Come on," Tobias said. "What you're doing is for them too."

Reluctantly Sam climbed into the seat next to him. The driver took off, throwing them back onto the hard vinyl seat.

Tobias took a new cell phone from his backpack, still in its box, and put it together.

"Who are you calling?" Sam asked.

"The Academy."

"What about people tracing the call?"

"It's a brand new phone. We have to check in. Lora, the

Professor, not to mention the rest of the last 13 . . . they're going to be worried."

"I hate to say it, but let them worry," Sam said with a frown.

Tobias stopped himself from putting the battery into the phone. "You *really* don't want me to contact them?"

"Nope," Sam said. "Let's just have one time when we can be sure that we haven't been followed, that we haven't been eavesdropped on. Let's just find Poh, find the Gear and get home quick as we can."

Tobias looked at the phone in his hands, then put all the pieces into his backpack.

"Thanks," Sam said.

"That's OK," Tobias replied. "Besides, you make a lot of sense. See—you're more ready for all this saving the world stuff than you think."

Sam smiled and watched the road bump past them. He hoped that the others would understand.

19

EVA

"This is where the tournament takes place," Lora said. "Just up here."

Eva pressed her nose up against the glass of the minivan, but could see nothing in the Turkish street that seemed like it might be the place until—

"Is that an Egyptian obelisk?" she asked.

Zara and Xavier moved around on the bench seat to get a look as they drove by.

"Yes," Lora said. "The Obelisk of Theodosius, the Ancient Egyptian obelisk of Pharaoh Tutmoses the Third."

"What's it doing here?" Eva asked.

"The Roman emperor Theodosius had it transported here and put up at the Hippodrome," Lora said.

"What's a hippodrome?" Zara asked.

"A sports arena, for chariot races, that kind of thing," Eva replied.

"Cool!" Zara said.

"That's correct," Lora said as their van pulled up. "Back in its heyday, it was estimated that the Hippodrome stands could hold a hundred thousand spectators."

"That's more than most sports stadiums *today!*" Xavier said.

"Uh-huh," Lora replied. "And we're going underneath what's left of it."

The Dreamer Doors complex underneath the site of the Hippodrome was a maze of rooms and tunnels that would have once served as stables and storage areas for the sports and races going on above. Eva and her fellow Dreamers marvelled at the history around them.

"Hey there!" a familiar voice called out to them.

Eva turned to see that Jedi had set up his computer gear in a well-lit cavern adorned with an intricate mosaic-tiled floor. A dozen staffers busied around him, helping set up computers and running cables and wires in and out of the room.

"Jedi, what are you doing here?" Eva asked.

"Running the show," he said. "Though don't expect any insider tips, I'm just supplying the computer grunt."

"Nice," Xavier said, checking out the setup.

"They're waiting for you," Jedi said to Lora, and she nodded and turned to the Dreamers.

"This way, no time to lose."

As they went past an outfitting station, Eva could see that the other teams were represented by the colours green, blue and yellow. Her team was red. All had the same type of Stealth Suits. All were hanging up, waiting for their contestants.

But surely one of those colours won't get used. Not now.

A woman saw Eva's tearful gaze and smiled knowingly. She slid the door closed as they walked on.

They were now in a long hall that had many rooms running off it, all filled with buzzing staff and students setting up for the tournament.

"It looks like they're getting ready for a long stay," Eva said.

"They plan for the long-term scenario," Lora said. "We could be here for up to a week."

"A big operation, no?" Zara said.

"They've been setting up all month," Lora replied. "Our quarters are down there."

Eva looked to where she was pointing, an offshoot from the hall lit up with red LED lighting along the floor.

"And through here," Lora said, the three of them hustling to keep up, "is the tournament space."

The wide double doors were open, revealing a round room with a domed roof. The centre was the size of a tennis court and divided into four segments with tiered seating for maybe a hundred people.

"Hey," Eva said, "there are still four sectors laid out, are all four teams competing?"

"Yes," a voice said. "Lora, good to see you."

"Hello, Zhang," Lora said. She turned to introduce the three Dreamers. "This is Zhang, the chairman of the Four Corners Competition."

"You competed against Lora and Sebastian," Eva said, recognizing the name.

"You know your Doors history," Zhang said with a smile. "And yes, I am pleased to say, the fourth quadrant have sent their back-up delegation. Ah, here they are now."

Eva watched as three Dreamers from the fourth quadrant, representing the Dreamer Academy that encompassed Asia and Oceania, strode into the room. Dressed in blue, they were clearly all seniors, and they looked at the three newcomers with what could have been pity. Then she noticed another six students heading over— the other two teams, also now dressed in their green and yellow colours.

They look older and more experienced too. What have we gotten ourselves into?

The twelve of them all looked at one another, weighing up their competition.

Eva didn't feel confident. Not even a tiny bit. But she didn't show it.

SAM

"The Angkor Wat temple was as tall as the Notre Dame church in Paris, and used as much stone as the great pyramid of Khufu," Tobias read from a tourist brochure as they left the outskirts of Siem Reap. "But it only took thirty-two years to build it. Big cathedrals in Europe would take three to four hundred years. And every surface is covered with exquisite carvings. They are the longest continuous sculptures in the world. The city of Angkor was the largest settlement in the pre-industrial world."

"You know, that really does sound amazing. But all I know is that we meet Poh at the temple at sunset," Sam said, looking up at the darkening afternoon sky.

"Then we'd better hurry," Tobias replied, and asked their tuktuk driver to speed up. He put the travel guide back in the holder behind the driver.

The driver did his best to avoid the potholes on the side roads they drove on to the main temple. The main roads were apparently deemed too dangerous due to recent civil unrest.

But there are no soldiers on this road. Not one.

All they could see were a few scared-looking families, fleeing the place in some kind of exodus away from densely populated areas.

They went around a bend in the forest road and slowed.

"What is it?" Tobias asked.

The driver pointed ahead—it was a roadblock.

Four guys stood in the road, armed with machine guns and waving at them to stop. Even from a distance, Sam thought that none of the armed men looked like they'd slept in days.

"Bandits, to rob us?" Tobias asked the driver.

"No," the driver replied over his shoulder. "They take you for big ransom later. This is trouble."

Sam noticed that Tobias had pulled his dart gun from his belt and kept it concealed behind the cover of the driver's seat.

"We don't have time for this," Tobias said, readying his weapon.

"And what can we do about it?" Sam said. "It's four armed guys against you and that peashooter."

"Sam," Tobias said out of the corner of his mouth. "When we stop, I want you to jump out. Have your Stealth Suit set to maximum shielding, then when they aim at you, go invisible. You got that?"

"And you?" Sam said, their ride almost at a complete stop on the bumpy road.

"I'll be the one doing all the shooting," Tobias said.

Sam jumped out as soon as the tuktuk driver brought them to a stop just ten metres in front of the gunmen.

He ran to the left.

The men shouted and a gunshot rang out.

He paused, looking their way.

Three of them aimed their weapons at him. The fourth was aimed up into the air—the shooter.

"That only warning!" the shooter shouted. "Stop now!"

Sam looked to Tobias at the same time he heard the now-familiar sound of the dart gun firing in quick succession.

Another gunshot rang out.

Sam fell backwards, feeling the force of the bullet as it struck him.

PFFT, PFFT.

"Sam!" Tobias said. His face appeared over Sam's, replacing the sky. "Are you OK?"

Sam nodded, out of breath and unable to speak.

"Come on," Tobias said, helping Sam to his feet. "You've just had the wind knocked out of you. We have to keep moving."

Tobias helped keep Sam upright as he got his breath back. They saw the bullet fall to the ground from where it had indented against Sam's Stealth Suit.

"That . . . was . . . close," Sam said, seeing the four bandits now unconscious on the forest track. Their driver stood stunned in the middle of the road.

"Close as they get," Tobias said, taking Sam back to the road and loading him into the tuktuk. "Let's roll."

Outside Angkor Wat they stopped at a street market and picked up some supplies. They'd found out that sunset was another half an hour off and Sam relaxed a little.

"What about weapons?" Sam asked Tobias.

"What about them?"

"Can we get some?" he asked. "I mean, looking at how spooked all these locals are, and the tourists looking like sleep-deprived zombies, there must be something here that we can buy."

"Let's find out."

Within five minutes they had purchased a real bounty, the sellers providing the goods from stashes hidden under the regular tourist gear. Sam bought a taser, Tobias a knife and they found several flares.

"Thankfully the place *is* so spooked," Tobias said, "that we can pretty much buy anything to protect ourselves right now."

"The bazookas must be all sold out."

"Bazookas? Meh. I think a tank would have been a good buy."

"A tank, yeah, nice."

Both of them now had a backpack full of food and water,

new flashlights and batteries. Still dressed in their Stealth Suits, Sam had turned his into shorts and a Hawaiian shirt.

"Yikes," Tobias said, seeing Sam's new outfit. "Reminds me of the hideous shirts that Jedi wears."

"I think I copied it from the memory of one he actually wore once," Sam said. He was lost in the thought for a moment, then looked up to the sky. "Come on, we've got one of the last 13 to meet."

"The Angkor Wat temple complex is the largest in the world," Tobias now read from his recently purchased guidebook. He looked up and added, "And it's also aligned on a ley line."

"Huh?" Sam said, not listening as he looked around in wonder. The temple itself was not the biggest in the world, Sam could tell without looking at a guidebook, but it had to be one of the most beautiful. It seemed to be on an island—the huge square patch of land it was built on was surrounded by a wide, square moat. On the island was the main temple building, set behind high walls, and the land outside the walls was covered with lush green trees. The ornately carved stone towers and outdoor galleries were striking against the trees and the water and the sky.

"Like that dream chamber we were in in Japan," Tobias said, "Angkor is along one of the most powerful ley lines. There is what's called a 'great circle' that many ancient structures are built on, or at least are within one degree of."

"That's, ah, spooky, I guess," Sam said, not wanting to seem uninterested. "So you're saying there's a hidden ring around the earth that conducts power through the planet?"

"Is that so hard to accept?" Tobias asked. "Sam, I'd think with all that you've learned these past few weeks, that the immense power of the earth would be the easiest idea to accept."

"Good point," Sam said. "I mean, it's not as far-fetched as being connected through our dreams to the location of Gears scattered around the world, is it?"

"And being connected to and finding other Dreamers," Tobias added.

"Yeah. OK, so there are ley lines that run through the earth. And people have built on them. Why?"

"That's one of the questions that I think the Dream Gate will answer."

"Great. A little more pressure." Sam looked at the horizon and what was left of the sun. Far off, gunfire crackled. Not a random shot, not the single crack of a hunter's rifle, but the rapid evil of assault rifles. People, fighting.

Sam was rattled. "More trouble—let's hope it's not coming this way."

"The world is in turmoil," Tobias said, pulling out the knife, hiding it in his right boot. "We can't get complacent or be too careful."

"I know, but wow . . ." Sam stood on the raised balcony of the outer gallery and looked out toward the entrance causeway over the moat. The tourists leaving the site for the day seemed oblivious to any threat.

Did they not hear it? That can't be normal around here, surely?

Sam looked around, watching as the remains of the day slipped away in the red-orange sunset.

"What do you think of when you see the sun?" Tobias asked.

Sam was silent. He was watching that view. Lost in it.

"Sam?"

"Fire." Sam watched the burning ball of gas, so far away through the solar system, yet big enough and close enough to heat the earth. "I think of fire."

"And what does that mean to you—how does it make you feel?"

Sam snapped out of his reverie and looked at his teacher. "You're asking how I feel about fire? About Toronto?"

"Yes."

"Fear. I'm still afraid of it. Probably always will be."

They were silent for a while. Then Tobias spoke. "How often do you think about your friend, Bill?"

Sam looked to his teacher. He'd been in his life when he'd lost his best friend from school, Bill, in a house fire in Toronto. Sam and Bill had been alone in the house. They'd been trapped. It had been a freak accident but that didn't make it any easier to deal with. Sam had thought of him almost every day since.

"Often," Sam said, looking back in the direction of the setting sun. "And I think of that night every time I see fire."

"How do you feel when you see the fire of Solaris?"

"Scared."

"And Solaris himself?"

"Angry."

"Not scared?"

"No. Not anymore. I've faced him already. I know he won't kill me, because he needs me. He may beat me to the Gears, to the Machine and the Gate, and that makes me angry, but I'm not scared of him. As long as he needs me, I know I'll be OK."

"But his fire . . ."

"His fire? Yes, I'm afraid of the fire—who wouldn't be? But I also know that he is controlling it, and because of that, I'm not as scared of it as I was when he was simply a nightmare from my dreams. And nothing scared me more than what really happened to my friend. How he must have felt."

Sam stood, squinting against the sunset. Suddenly there was movement, coming toward them. A big mass, as high as the wall of the temple.

"What is it?" Tobias said, standing next to him.

It took Sam a little while to make him out, but then he knew at once who it was. He'd dreamed this.

Sam smiled.

The next Dreamer was here. Number four.

Poh.

ALEX

"**W**hat's happening?" Alex asked, breathless from running up to the command bridge. Hans was there. The ship's crew looked spooked. The German Guardians had their weapons drawn.

"That," Hans said. He pointed to a couple of dots in the sky.

"What are they?" Alex asked.

"Drones," Hans replied. "They've found us. They just did a fly-by, and now they're coming back around out there to come in on an attack run."

"Drones?" Alex said, looking at the aircraft as they banked around in the sky to turn toward them. "Who do they belong to?"

"Stella," Hans said.

"Why don't you just go stealth?" Alex said.

"We *have*," Hans replied. "That's why I think it's her. She's the one most likely to have the hardware to see through our invisibility tech."

"Then what do we do?" Alex said. He could see that the crewman at the wheel was turning the ship around so that the front, the bow, was to the attacking drones, presenting a smaller target.

"We brace ourselves," Hans said. "And we fight!" He motioned his armed men to go out to the decks so that they could counter-attack the aircraft.

"But not you, Alex!" Hans said. "You must go to the engine room. Now, go!"

"But—"

"It's the safest place. Go!"

Hans shoved Alex toward the stairs and he raced down, meeting Dr. Kader on the landing, and together they went down to the engine room. It was in the centre of the ship, below the waterline, with hallways and storage at either side that would form protection against their attackers. A crewman was there, working hard to get more speed out of the ship's engines.

"Can we help?" Alex asked.

The man just shook his head, leaning back and rubbing grime and grease from his hands, then motioning them to a small area with a few chairs bolted to the floor and arranged around a small table.

Dr. Kader sat down, his heavy leather bag filled with his most precious notes and artifacts clutched tight across his chest. The lights above still flashed red, and the alarm rang loudly in Alex's ears as he took a seat.

And waited.

What will it be like, when those drones start shooting at us?

What will happen to the ship?

"It'll be alright, Alex," Dr. Kader said, reading Alex's expression. "This is a strong vessel—the hull is made for breaking through ice, the steel is strong. We will be OK."

Alex nodded.

Then the sound of gunfire pierced the air.

Even down in the engine room, four levels below the deck and with the two big engines running at full speed, Alex could make out the sound of the German Guardians' machine guns. It was not the pitter-patter sound of calculated shots. It was a frenzy.

Are they shooting at those aircraft? Could a small hand-held weapon possibly shoot one of those things from the sky?

For a moment, Alex's mind drifted back to the time when he was in Berlin, racing to help Sam, who was trapped in a fierce firefight between Stella's and Hans' forces.

And it's still the same. They're still fighting each other.

KLAP-BOOM!

The explosion rocked the *Ra*, the sound waves shuddering through the ship, shaking everything loose to the floor.

KLAP-BLOOSH!

"What was *that?*" Dr. Kader asked the crewman.

"A missile," Alex replied. "One hit the deck above. Another hit the water."

"Missiles?" Dr. Kader said.

Alex nodded.

A radio squawked and the crewman picked it up, listened, then rushed from the room saying something about having to fight a fire topside.

"You have heard a missile before?" Dr. Kader asked.

"Yes," Alex said, recalling the time he was on the Enterprise helicopter that had been shot from the sky. "I had a close call."

Dr. Kader looked grim as anxious minutes ticked by.

"It's OK," Alex said, standing up. "Listen . . ."

Aside from the incessant alarm, there was nothing but the sound of the engines working hard.

"You think that they're gone?" Dr. Kader asked.

Alex waited, shrugged, then went over to the ship's internal radio system and picked up the receiver. It was dead, there was not even static on the line.

"Should we go back up?" Dr. Kader said. "See the damage?"

"I don't know," Alex said, looking at the door that led to the steel stairs.

"Maybe we need to evacuate—we could be sinking," Dr. Kader said. "I mean, we might not know . . ."

A shiver ran down Alex's spine at the thought of having to leave the large ship in the middle of the ocean and make do on a tiny life raft.

"You said this ship was built strong," Alex said. "You changing your mind now?"

"Ships and fires don't mix," Dr. Kader said.

Alex swallowed hard. He looked at the engines. Each

was the size of a single bed, each shiny and well maintained and vibrating fast as it continued to produce its maximum power. "We can't risk it," he said. "Those aircraft might just have passed and are doing a big turn through the sky like they did before, getting ready to make another pass at us."

"So we wait," Dr. Kader said, leaning back and clutching his case.

Alex sat down on the chair and braced himself, preparing for the worst.

SAM

Poh rode into the Angkor Wat temple complex on an elephant. The majestic beast swayed gently as it walked in with huge, lolling steps. As Poh slid from its back, the enormous animal stopped to drink water from the moat. Poh threw open the huge baskets on the animal's back to bring it food. He scurried around the animal, tending to it, checking it over, talking to it and giving it a pat on the head and a treat of bananas.

"It's beautiful," Sam said to Poh, coming over to stand by the elephant.

"She is magnificent," Poh replied. "I call her Dara—it means star, or precious, in my language."

"I'm Sam," Sam said, "and this is my friend, Tobias." He pointed to Tobias who waved genially as he strolled over, his casual manner concealing his alertness.

"You are much taller in person," Poh said to Sam. Poh himself was only up to Sam's shoulder, slightly built, wearing oversized shorts and a sloppy yellow T-shirt, which was ripped in places and looked like it had never had a wash. "In my dream, we were looking at one another eye-to-eye."

"You've dreamed about me?" Sam asked.

"Many times." Poh smiled. "Every night for these past twenty nights."

"That's incredible," Sam said, and he looked to Tobias, who shrugged. "Poh, have you dreamed of us finding a Gear?"

"Gear?" Poh said. He picked up some tightly bound branches, undid the twine and fed it to the elephant, stroking it gently as he did so. It had now attracted a large crowd of the last tourists who posed with it and took happy snaps. Tobias did his best to keep the crowd at bay.

"A brass disc," Sam said, keeping close to Poh. "A brass disc with teeth, or cogs, all around the edges. Like the gear on a bicycle."

"Ah, yes," Poh said. "A gear."

"Yes, you have seen it?" Sam replied.

"I have seen plenty of bicycles. But I only ride elephants."

"I mean a brass disc, in your dreams. That's what you are supposed to have a dream about."

"No," Poh replied. "I have not seen such a thing. But I do know what you mean. I will dream of it soon."

"We need to find it."

"I know."

Sam was confused. "How do you know?"

"Because we had this conversation, in my dream," Poh said. "Which is lucky for you, because now you are saved the trouble of explaining my destiny to me, because I already know." He beamed a dazzling smile, displaying unbelievably white teeth as he tied an old rope around the foot of the elephant and tethered it to a metal stake that he pushed into the ground.

"I don't think that rope or stake will hold her," Sam said, imagining the elephant would have no trouble pulling out the stake or breaking the rope and simply walking off.

"It's not supposed to," Poh replied. "She knows to stay here, with me, and this is just a reminder to her, so that in the night she doesn't wander too far. She is a good elephant—she never tries to run off."

"I see," Sam said.

"We will camp here," Poh replied. Guards were dispersing the tourists, emptying the temple for the night.

"I'm not sure we are allowed to," Sam said, as a couple of security officers walked over their way.

"I will talk to them," Poh said, his voice peaceful. He ambled over and spoke quietly to the guards, pointing back to the elephant and his two new friends. The security guys nodded and continued to empty the temple complex of the remaining sightseers.

"OK?" Tobias asked Poh.

"We can stay," Poh replied.

"They don't mind?"

"Why would they mind?" Poh said, and he went to a large backpack and brought out equipment to make camp.

Sam and Tobias shared a look and this time Sam shrugged. "Stranger things have happened, I guess."

24

EVA

The roar of the crowd was deafening as Eva, Zara and Xavier re-entered the arena, this time dressed in their red Stealth Suits.

At least we look the part now.

Xavier waved to the spectators, who filled every seat in the four sections. He smiled and called out to well-wishers, looking every inch like he belonged there. Zara had been swept up in his enthusiasm during their prep time and was equally as charming.

And that's our team covered for being good sports, then. Let's hope they get focused in the competition so we can find those Gears and get out of there. Meanwhile I've got to fend the others off for the prize.

Eva glanced nervously at the other competitors as they shook hands and smiled for the official photographs. A dark-haired boy from the South-West quadrant leaned over to her. "My name is Juan, a pleasure to meet you, Eva," he said, shaking her hand vigorously. "I look forward to beating your team in the Doors. We may not be last 13, but we are powerful Dreamers, all the same."

Eva looked into his face and saw no malice, only what she suspected was an overdeveloped sense of competition and quite possibly jealousy. "I look forward to proving you wrong, Juan." She forced herself to beam her best smile.

Zara appeared to be getting along famously with one of the South-East team, laughing at some joke the small girl from Indonesia was telling her. Xavier was already surrounded by a gaggle of admirers and was signing autographs.

How come I'm the one who gets the unfriendly guy?

She sighed and tried to ooze confidence and edged toward Lora for support.

"It's OK," Lora soothed, reading Eva's expression. "Friendly banter and competition is all part of the game. Stay focused on your mission to keep the construct open for the others."

"You're right," Eva said. "I will, I'll do my best."

"Of course you will," Lora replied. "That's why we chose you."

Without much more ceremony, which Eva suspected was largely orchestrated by Lora who seemed as eager as she for the contest to begin, Zhang announced the prize to find that year was a small handheld mirror. He displayed an image of the ornate silver object to all the teams, then promptly announced the Four Corners Competition open.

They were ushered to their respective seats and technicians fussed around them, getting them ready. The

North-East quadrant would be driving the dream as the previous year's winners. Their leader was a tall, wiry girl called Imena. She smiled broadly at Eva as they settled into their chairs for the competition.

They obviously know who we are. Does that mean they'll go easy on us or . . . ?

"Remember, Dreamers," Zhang was saying, "you must trust the construct—let go of your subconscious mind and let it guide you to your prize. Fight hard, fight fair and may the best Dreamers win!"

The crowd burst into applause.

Eva gave Lora a final look before they went under. The last thing she remembered was seeing Lora's face smiling back at her and watching the flags waving high above their heads fade into a dreamy haze.

SAM

"What is it?" Sam asked, worried. He'd watched and listened as Tobias spoke on the phone. He'd insisted on touching base with the Professor but Sam could see that whatever news he had was worrying.

"It's the Dreamer Doors—" Tobias began.

"Eva?"

"She's . . ." Tobias looked like he was struggling to explain it. "She's fine, they all are, but someone has taken over the dream construct."

"How do they know? Why doesn't Lora just wake them up?"

"They can't. They realized something was wrong almost immediately but it was already too late to wake them. They're working with all the technicians now to try to bring them out. Until then, all the competitors are still in there. They probably don't even realize something is wrong. But with unknown elements involved, who knows what might happen. We have to trust that they'll get them all out."

"Stella?" Sam shuddered.

"Maybe."

"It has to be Stella! Those Tesla coils she was researching—she can access the Dreamscape with them."

"No, it can't be the coils, we've got those locked down. Shiva's there, along with a couple of dozen armed Enterprise Agents. No way would they let them fall into Stella's hands again."

"Then how else is she doing it?"

"Some way that we haven't discovered yet."

"And Eva? What will happen to her and the others?"

"She'll remain asleep until she finds her own way out of the construct."

"What?"

"That's how a dream construct works—once you are in there, the only safe way out of it is to choose the exit yourself."

Sam didn't know what to say. He felt sick in his stomach for his friends.

"That's why dream constructs are not used in any other circumstance, and why the Dreamer Doors are accessed by only the most capable Dreamers."

"But Eva, Zara and Xavier weren't chosen because they were the most-skilled Dreamer students but because we wanted them to use the construct to help find the missing Gears, isn't that right?" Sam queried.

Tobias looked worried. He nodded.

"No!" Sam said and stormed off. He grit his teeth and clenched his fists.

What can I do? What can we do?

Surely Lora can figure it out, the Professor too. But how?

"There is trouble?" Poh asked. Concern creased his face.

Sam looked at the newest Dreamer. Poh's peaceful eyes stared back.

"Some of my friends are in trouble," Sam said.

"Can you help them?" Poh asked.

"I don't think I can," Sam replied.

Can I?

"Maybe you can help them find a solution," Poh said, "in your dream, tonight? You can talk to them, just as you talked to me in my dreams and told me to come here."

Sam was taken aback. "Maybe I can . . ."

Poh smiled.

"What did we talk about in your dream?" Sam asked Poh.

Poh looked back at his elephant which was now relaxing after being fed and watered.

"Life, family, dreams," Poh said. "The last thing that you were asking me about was fear."

"Fear?"

"Yes. You explained that you were afraid of fire. I told you my fear—that I was afraid of stepping on cracks. Such a silly superstition, I don't know why I let it bother me. Sometimes when the big things feel like too much, the smaller things become easier to fear. Right?"

Sam looked down at Poh's feet. He stood on the cobbled ground of the temple complex, lined with seams and cracks.

"See," Poh said, looking up from his feet and meeting Sam's gaze. There was a sureness there that Sam took comfort in. "You helped me in my dream. Now you can help others."

ALEX

"This is a map made in 1513, known as the Piri Reis map," Dr. Kader said. "Piri Reis' own commentary indicates that some of his source maps were from the time of Alexander the Great in 332 BC."

"Ah, yeah, that's cool," Alex replied. It had been five minutes since the missiles had gone off. Five minutes, and nothing since. The alarms still sounded and the lights still flashed. The engines still ran at full power. No one, not Hans, nor any of the crew, had reappeared.

But all was quiet.

Too quiet.

But Alex could see that Ahmed Kader's default position in times of stress was to talk, to get his mind off the here and now. So he'd taken some papers from his bag and was showing them to Alex, who did his best to feign interest in the face of a history lecture.

"It's more than cool," Dr. Kader said with a chuckle. "It is a pre-modern world map compiled in 1513, long before one could calculate longitude with any certainty."

"So you're telling me that . . ." Alex's voice trailed off as he heard what he thought was more gunfire, but it turned out to be one of the engines starting to backfire. He went over to it. "What do we do?"

Dr. Kader joined him.

The engine was starting to shake on its mounts, something was clearly wrong with it. Thick black-blue smoke started to pour from it.

"How do we shut it down?" Alex said.

"I don't know!" Ahmed gasped, clearly out of his depth.

Alex put a rag over his face against the fumes and raced around the engine, looking for any sign that there may be some kind of switch to press.

A key!

He reached for it—

"No!" the engineer yelled from the doorway.

Alex looked at him. He looked like he'd stepped out of a coal mine, covered head to toe in dark black soot. He raced over to Alex and instead of killing the engine he pulled a lever to turn it down.

"If it shuts down completely," the crewman said, taking heaving breaths, "we won't get it started again."

"What's happening up there?" Alex asked him.

The engineer was already using a wrench to tighten bolts on the engine. "They got one aircraft, shot it right from the sky," he replied. "But the other one is still up there."

"Why isn't it attacking again?"

"Who knows," the guy said, working hard to get the

engine running properly.

At least the smoke has stopped pouring out.

"And the *Ra*?" Dr. Kader said.

"She's banged up," the engineer said. "One more direct hit and we'll be swimming to shore."

Alex swallowed hard. "Should we stay down here?" he asked.

The engineer remained silent as he worked.

"I will stay until Hans says otherwise," Dr. Kader said, sitting down at the table again.

Alex crouched down to the engineer. "Can I do something to help you?"

The guy looked up and wiped grime and sweat from his face. "OK, sure, hand me that toolbox over there," he said, pointing.

Alex rushed over, happy for something productive to do, the deck underfoot unstable as the *Ra* was being churned in the ocean, the waves rocking it from side-to-side.

"This one?" Alex asked, holding a small red toolbox he grabbed from a shelf.

The guy nodded.

Alex headed back.

And never made it.

KLAP-BOOM!

The missile struck as the *Ra*'s side rocked above the water, hitting the ship dead-on. The sound was like nothing Alex had ever heard.

The force was enough to knock him off his feet and slam him hard against the deck, his head bouncing off something metal, the darkness of unconsciousness washing over him.

27

SAM

The camp fire was small and hidden behind a little rock wall that they had made, the elephant apparently having a similar disposition toward fire as Sam. Poh placed an earthenware bowl inside the fire, settling it onto half of the coals. He loaded it with rice and a vegetable curry that he'd made from ingredients he took from a bamboo basket.

Sam settled in, sitting between Poh and Tobias, the elephant's eyes gleaming in the dark background as it ate branches collected from the forest bordering the temple complex.

"There's said to be less than four hundred left in the wild," Poh said, sitting there close to the fire and dishing out bowls of food.

"Four hundred what?" Sam asked.

Poh pointed to the elephant. "And even less than that in captivity."

"I thought a country like Cambodia would have more than that?" Sam said. By the orange glow of the fire and the light of the full moon he could see its mighty form, chomping at the branches of lush foliage.

"They're hunted for their ivory," Poh said, sitting next to Sam, "and sometimes their meat is taken too, but that is perhaps seen as a bonus for the poachers. The presence of hunters has made the remaining elephants extremely wary of humans," he explained. "So they have learned to be constantly on the move. We have plenty of natural habitat for the elephant population to recover, but it is hard without political will and the money to fund such protection."

"I'm sorry to hear that," Sam said, "I wish we could do something to help. Maybe after . . ."

"I hope so. I was born in Phnom Penh but my grandparents were from this district. It was their wish, a long time ago, to care for the elephants," Poh said. "So my parents told me."

"Are your grandparents still around?" Tobias asked.

Poh shook his head. "They were killed."

"Who killed them?" Sam said quietly.

"The thugs who once tried to rule my country many years ago," Poh said. "They took over by force and by the time we had stopped them, our country had suffered a great deal."

Sam knew who Poh was talking about. He remembered from history class—a group who had controlled the country nearly forty years before and killed many thousands of innocent civilians. It made him grit his teeth, thinking how awful that was, and how terrible it would be if such a thing were to happen again.

"How did you get this elephant here?" Tobias asked, gently changing the subject.

"Dara was an orphan," Poh said. "Like many of the others I care for, her parents were killed. We take in the elephants, they grow up, we release them back to the wild so that they breed and live free. Some of them are killed, we take in their orphans. It's a circle, you see? The past couple of months have been the worst—killings all over the forests. Something has changed in the air, people are going crazy. More than ever."

Tobias gave Sam a long, meaningful look.

The world's in chaos because of the prophecy, because of the race to the Dream Gate.

"I took in three new orphans that are back at the nursery," Poh continued. "Usually it's only two or three per *year*. The times seem to . . . they are getting bad, very bad."

"We're working on that," Sam said, a twist of urgency in his stomach.

"We're trying to fix things," Tobias added. "In some ways, what you're going to help us with will help them in the long run. Do you know why we're here?"

"Yes, I dreamed about it. I know," Poh said quietly.

"You know?" Tobias asked again.

"I know I have to go with you," Poh said. He patted his elephant. "And I know that soon it will be revealed to me where it is that we have to go."

EVA

*W*ow, so this is what the construct is like. Sort of just like any other dream. Huh.

The team had awoken in Spain—all the teams being required to begin in a European country, all similarly distant from wherever the prize was hidden. Eva recognized the spires of Barcelona immediately and as they ran down the city streets, they quickly learned to recognize doors that looked just that bit different from any other.

"Let's go through a white one together and get somewhere different," Xavier said. "We need to shake things up to start our search."

"OK," Zara agreed. "How about Stonehenge?"

"Good choice," Eva said. They were all going to work together and not argue about destinations. And going to places heavily connected to ancient cultures and Dreaming history seemed like a good start.

They walked up to a door on a small side street. "This should be one," Eva said. "Ready?"

Zara and Xavier nodded.

"On three," Eva said. "One, two, three."

They were standing in the freezing wind and rain in southern England, right among the stones themselves, panting for breath from their run up the hill.

"Hey!" A security guard spotted them almost instantly.

"Really? Imena set up security *here?*" Xavier exclaimed. They started running, almost laughing with the exhilaration as they began to lift off the ground.

"We're flying!" Eva cried. "This is so amazing!"

"More like bounding," Zara exclaimed. "But I love it!"

They were soon out of range of any security personnel and stopped to take stock.

"OK, as agreed, we split up so you guys can chase down your Gears," Eva said. "You both stick together for now as its likely the Gears are in the same place. Reach out to the Gears with your subconscious Dreamer mind and follow your gut."

"And the meeting point?" Xavier said.

"The Eiffel Tower," Eva said, "two hours from now, we'll see what our progress is then."

"*Oui*, it is agreed," Zara said, taking Xavier's hand to race off down the hillside, looking for a white door nearby.

OK, now I need to find that mirror.

Mirror, mirror on the . . . that's not going to help.

Hmm.

Eva sat down on the wet grass and closed her eyes.

Focus. There are clues within the prize and within the construct.

The image of the mirror swam before her eyes. She slowed down her breathing and thought of nothing else but the mirror. Gradually she began to remember the exact design on the back of it. There was some kind of pattern.

Aztec?

Eva bounded across the fields until she found a farmhouse where she knew there would be a white door. Walking up to a large barn, she grasped the door handle, and firmly planted her destination in her mind as she opened the door and walked through.

In a heartbeat she was in the Valley of Mexico, standing in radiant sunshine on top of the plateau. But in the wink of an eye, a shadow passed over the sun.

That wasn't a cloud? But then what was it—a construct blip?

As she looked around, the sun blinked out again and again. Startled, she gazed up and saw black streaks swirling across the sky, growing larger every minute—

And heading straight for her.

SAM

Sam did not sleep but Poh slumbered on next to him. Tobias too, for a while. He woke when Sam stoked the fire and added another large log.

"Sorry to wake you," Sam said, staring at the fire, looking at the hot coals that burned brightly, the fresh oxygen invigorating them. The log crackled and spat.

"That's fine," Tobias replied. "I was having a bad dream anyway."

"Is something bad going to happen now?" Sam's face creased in a frown.

"I'm not sure," Tobias said, sitting up and opening a bottle of water. "But I doubt very much it was a true dream—I rarely have them now, just hints and memories."

"Why?"

"Why don't I true dream? Because I'm not following my path, not following where my own dreams take me," he said. "Since this started, I've been in your world. I'm steering my dreams to follow you, following *your* destiny. That's where I belong right now—right here, with you."

"You're sure about that?" Sam asked.

Tobias nodded. "I was assigned to be your teacher, to watch over you, and I've stuck with that since."

They sat in silence a while, the brilliant starry sky above, the crackling fire below.

A startling gunshot echoed through the forest to the east, over the moat. Another salvo snapped off. Three shots, closer than before.

"Bandits," Poh said, sitting up, instantly alert from his slumber. "We should be careful."

"Did you . . . ?" Sam said.

"Dream?" Poh asked.

Sam nodded. Waited.

Poh broke into a toothy grin. "Yes! We must find . . . wait." He looked puzzled, trying to recall something. "Snakes! We have to find snakes!"

By the light of the full moon, the inscription carved into the square slab of paving stone was revealed.

They were standing about fifty metres north from where they'd made camp, where Poh had led them to an area of thick undergrowth. They cleared roots and soil and moss away by hand to reveal the carved paving stone, set among a cluster of similar stones.

"What does it mean?" Sam asked.

"It means that just like meeting you here," Poh said, "my dreams are continuing to come true. It is . . . amazing."

"What's next?" Sam asked.

Poh scratched his head and looked around. Crouching down, he knocked on the paving stone, his ear close to it. He repeated the process, tapping and listening to the paving stones around the central one.

"I was stupid," Tobias said under his breath. "We need a dream reading machine—we came here ill-prepared, I should have brought one. I can call in, have one flown in by tomorrow."

More gunfire filled the air, a lethal staccato across the sky. It seemed closer here and Sam felt the urge to gather the three of them and the elephant and run to the west.

We could come back tomorrow, in the daylight, when we have the additional support of the Guardians.

"I remember now!" Poh said. "We go down—under the stone."

"Down?" Tobias asked.

"Under the stone," Poh repeated. He pulled a knife from his belt and prised it into an edge. Nothing.

Centuries of weather and neglect had locked the stone in place. He worked the blade along the seam of the paver, cleaning it out, digging into the space between the seam that was no thicker than the blade, working like this on each of the four edges so that it was eventually freed. He looked up to the others as he knocked on the paver again, then on those adjacent to it.

"It's hollow!" Sam said, now hearing the difference. "There's a cavity underneath."

With more cleaning and prying, and with the effort of the three of them working together, the stone lifted up like a trapdoor. It was a lid. It revealed a small, square, stone-lined space below it. A slight breeze came up from a tunnel just big enough to wriggle through in a tight squeeze.

Sam stuck his head down into the space and cast his flashlight around. It was a smooth stone-lined drain, a small trickle of water at the bottom, running north. He'd fit in there, Poh too.

But definitely not Tobias.

"The Gear we are searching for is down here," Poh said. "In my dream I saw that it was placed here for safekeeping."

"You watched it being hidden?" Sam asked.

"Yes. It was like I was watching a movie. It was more than five hundred years ago, when Cambodia was in a state of change. I remember my father telling me stories about adventurers from Spain and Portugal who came to our country and helped overthrow the foreign powers that once controlled it. They freed us from the chaos."

"Do you remember who they were?" Sam asked.

"I was not sure," Poh said, "until I saw *this*." He smiled as he pointed at the carving on the paving stone. "But now I know for certain. Their names were Ruiz and Veloso."

"The initials on the stone," Sam said, running his fingers over the engraving. "R and V. *They* put it here."

"For safekeeping against the chaos," Tobias said, "and for us to find. Anything else?"

"Yes, there's a big elephant down there," Poh said, as though that would be the most ordinary thing.

"Elephant?" Sam asked, poking his head down the hole again. "I don't think an elephant could fit down here, Poh."

Poh simply shrugged and smiled.

Another volley of gunfire emanated from the forest. Poh's elephant trumpeted loudly, stamping its feet. Poh looked back toward their campfire.

"She's getting angry at the noise—she thinks it's poachers," he said. "I want to check on her before we go on our adventure. OK?"

Sam and Tobias nodded, walking back with Poh to their camp.

"So who made this Gear we are looking for?" Poh asked as he checked over his elephant.

"Some say Leonardo da Vinci," Tobias replied. "Some say it was made much earlier."

"Sixteenth century at the latest," Sam added as he

stood and waited for Poh to finish checking Dara, her eyes shining in the dark. "It's thought that these Gears were secretly adapted to form parts of devices, which were then hidden away around the globe, via explorers taking them on their travels."

"But—that is not true?" Poh asked. "You do not sound so sure."

More crackling gunfire rang out.

"Maybe not," Tobias said, looking to Sam.

"We think—well, Tobias and I were talking about it on the flight here—that it makes more sense if, on the death of da Vinci, the Gears to the Bakhu Machine were split up and given to thirteen prominent Dreamers, who then made sure that they were hidden away."

"Wow," Poh said. "And one of these Gears is somewhere near here?"

"If that's what your dream is telling you, yes," Tobias said. "But it's time for you to hustle. I'll wait up here, keep an eye out. You two go on."

"You're sure?" Sam said.

Tobias smiled. "Yes, Sam. This is your destiny, remember, not mine. You and Poh go, I'll hold things down here. Good luck."

Sam nodded, and one after the other, the pair of them walked back to the upturned slab and went headfirst into the square hole, dropping down into the drain. They began wriggling their way north, following the flowing water.

ALEX'S DREAM

"**E**va?" I ask. Eva looks like she is running from someone. We are on a city street. She keeps looking back, as though checking to see if she is being followed.

"Surprised to see me?" Eva replies over her shoulder.

I struggle to keep up.

"Who are you running from?" I ask.

"Oh, the usual," she grins.

"Where are we?"

"You don't want to know."

"Ah, I do," I say. We round a corner, and Eva leads us into a building. It's a restaurant at the base of a tall office block. Eva watches out the window. Soon, Stella runs by, Matrix too and a bunch of rogue Enterprise Agents. "What are they doing?"

"Chasing you." She stares at me.

"Me?" I look around. "Where are we?"

"In your dream."

"In my what?"

"Look, Alex, I'm sorry, but I can't stay long," Eva says. "I have a mission."

"But how are you in my dream?"

"I'm in the competition—the Dreamer Doors, and then you dragged me in here," she says.

"In here?"

"Your dream. I'm in the Dreamscape. They have a bridge to it, that they call the construct. We're in it to find the Gears that have been taken from us."

"Yeah, I get all that, but I still don't see how you're here—"

"Shh!"

Eva points and we duck down as Stella circles back, looking for us, dart gun drawn. Matrix is right next to her.

"No!" Eva whispers to me, holding me back. "You can't fight them, not now. I can't get caught."

"I really hate that guy," I say, fire burning in my eyes as I imagine running out there and wrestling the gun from Matrix's grip and shooting him with it.

"Alex," Eva says, "why are we *here*?"

"I . . ." I look around. "I don't even know where here is."

"Seattle."

"Oh, really?" I look around my home town from the view out the restaurant window. "I—I've got no idea. I didn't even know that I was asleep."

"Well, you are, and you brought me in here."

"How?"

"Look, they're going," Eva says.

We watch as Stella and Matrix disappear down the street.

"Look, Alex, I can't stay here with you," Eva says. "But

maybe you came here in your dream because it's a familiar, comfortable place. And you dragged me in because you need help. Is that right?"

"Maybe. I'm not sure."

"Where are you?"

"Floating . . . I'm at sea."

Eva turns, listening to something that I cannot hear.

"Alex, I'm sorry, but I must go," Eva says, already heading out the door. "If you need to get out of here—take a white door, and think of where you need to be . . ."

"Eva, wait!" I run after her, pulling open the door to the restaurant and bursting onto the Seattle street. But she's not there. No one is there.

And it's no longer Seattle.

"Ah, Alex," Hans says. "Take a seat, please."

I turn around and do a double take. He's standing in a wood-panelled dining room. Hans is up at one end, motioning me to sit at the other. As I do so, I peer out a window. We are a couple of storeys up, in a house that could well be a castle, and there are sprawling grounds outside.

"My chef has worked at all the best restaurants," Hans says, picking up his cutlery to eat the duck on the plate in front of him. "And he's always on call, should you want something made. How's your steak?"

"Steak?"

Hans motions to the plate at the table setting where he wants me to sit.

"Where are we?" I ask as I take my place at the table.

"My home, in Germany," Hans says, pouring himself a wine.

"But how . . ."

"We're in a dream, Alex," Hans says, matter of fact. "Must you keep asking the same question? Really? Take it from me—enjoy your dreams whenever you can. Go on, try the steak."

"It's good," I reply. Truth is, it is *amazing*. A rib-eye cut on the bone, cooked over a charcoal grill and filling up the entire plate.

"You seem preoccupied," Hans says, sipping wine. "Is there something that we are not providing?"

"No," I say. "It's not that. Not at all. I just feel . . . tired. Tired, in a dream? How does that work? And for what it's worth, I don't think I've ever dreamed like this—where I'm so aware that I'm dreaming. It's weird."

"You're getting better at it," Hans said, eating his meal. "That's good."

I nod, but truth is, I'm feeling lonely and sad. I'm worried about my friends—about Shiva, my mother and what the rest of the 13 are doing. They are out there, battling to win the race, and here I am, on some multi-million dollar superyacht, sailing who knows where, with everything I could ever want at my beck and call, and yet none of it is what I really need.

"Maybe dessert will cheer you up," Hans says through a

mouthful of food. "But I understand that you would be very tired, with all that you have been through, and if you want to go to bed at any time, please do so."

"Yeah, thanks," I say, still feeling like I am in a daze. I lay down my knife and fork as I stand up. "I think I should go. I think I should figure out what this dream is supposed to be."

"Ah," Hans says. "That's good. You have temptation before you, in food, in friends—oh yes, I saw you talking to Eva before. But you are aware of a bigger game at play here. You can steer your dreams, Alex. So go ahead. Ask yourself. What is it you want, you need, to know?"

"I . . . I want to know where we are headed."

"Antarctica," Hans replied. "We're headed to Antarctica."

31

SAM

Sam watched Poh's feet ahead of him, wriggling forward in the dark drain, for nearly half an hour. Sam's arms and legs were aching from squeezing along on his stomach doing a commando crawl.

Who knew this was so hard? We've probably only gone a few hundred metres. Geez.

Sam shook his head and followed Poh farther into the drain, a face-first and belly-down wriggle, following the water and Poh's dream.

"Argh!" Sam said as something crawled over his hand.

"What is it?" Poh asked, stopping for a moment.

"Something just crawled over my hand," Sam said.

"Just a little bug," Poh said and continued moving.

"You can see them?" Sam asked, seeing little more on the floor of the dark drain than water and slime.

"Oh yes," Poh said. "Just a few little bugs."

Great, just great. Saving the world, one bug at a time.

As Sam muttered to himself, suddenly he heard Poh call out.

"Sam, look out!"

Too late Sam noticed Poh's feet had disappeared from view. He crashed down into a chamber below, as Poh must have just done, landing on his back and knocking the air out of his lungs. Poh helped him to his feet and by the light of the flashlight, he could make out that they were in a room barely high enough for him to stand in. His legs burned and he gratefully stretched out his limbs.

"Now it is better to be short, ha!" Poh grinned.

"Very true, my friend, you got me there," Sam laughed.

They gazed around the chamber, full of carved reliefs in stone—dozens, hundreds of elephants going to war against an invading force.

"What is this place?" Sam wondered.

"I'm not sure," Poh said, studying the scenes with his flashlight.

"Did you dream of it?"

"I can't be sure." Poh sighed.

"You dreamed of an elephant down here. These are elephants."

"In my dream it was a big elephant," Poh said. "The biggest I've ever seen."

They were silent as they continued to inspect the chamber. The room was square, perhaps four metres on all sides. The water tunnel ended there, and others did too—some at head height, others at different heights from the floor. At each of the four main points of the compass, there were the same-sized drains as the one they'd just travelled through.

"This must have been part of the water system of the city," Sam said.

"Yes," Poh said. "The water canals and catchments of Angkor are what made it the greatest pre-industrial city. This water, though, that made the city, was also its downfall."

"Because of drought?"

"Yes." Poh stopped, then put his head into another of the water supply ducts that was at around waist level. "This way—it's this way!"

Sam could hardly reply before Poh had climbed in and disappeared down the water tunnel. He crawled after him, arms pulling forward, then legs, the movement as constricted as before, his back aching.

"I'm following Poh from Phnom Penh," Sam said, slightly breathless.

"Yep," Poh called out from in front.

"Wouldn't want to say that ten times fast."

"Why?"

"Bit of a tongue twister, isn't it?" Sam stopped his movement and laughed, and found he could not stop, tears welling up in his eyes.

"Sam—are you alright?" Poh's concern brought Sam back to earth.

"Nothing, just a joke. I'm sorry, I'm so exhausted."

"Oh. Hahaha." Poh kept on moving, fast, as though he

were not the least bit tired.

They continued on, crawling through what was now a dry tunnel, until—

Poh dropped from sight and landed with an almighty crash.

"Poh?" Sam called out. "Poh! You OK?"

Sam was in complete darkness. Poh had been leading with the flashlight when he'd dropped out of the tunnel and the light had gone out. By the time that Sam had scrambled along and felt the edge of the drain, he could not see or hear his newest friend. "Poh?"

"It's OK," Poh said. "It's quite a drop, though."

"Can you find the flashlight?" Sam called down.

"Yes."

"Can you switch it on so that I can see?"

"No," Poh replied.

"Sorry?"

"It's broken," Poh said. "But hang on a moment."

Sam waited where he was, hunched up on his stomach in the square tunnel, unable to turn or change positions in the tight confines.

SPARK!

A small bright blue eruption of sparks lit the room for a second.

SPARK. SPARK.

Poh, standing directly below Sam, was sparking a magnesium fire starter.

"OK, I saw the floor," Sam said. "I'm coming down."

Sam wriggled forward, arms outstretched, and dropped down with an unceremonious crash.

Poh helped him up and sparked the magnesium again and again as they looked around.

"This way," Poh said.

"Do you know where we are?" Sam asked, his outstretched hand on Poh's shoulder as they navigated the darkness.

"I think so," Poh replied.

By the light of the sparks they shuffled along what turned out to be a large cave of sorts, and Poh stopped at the bottom of a stone staircase.

"It's up here," Poh said.

They climbed in darkness on their hands and knees, the stairs being nearly twice as tall as any Sam had ever seen.

Are we in the land of giants?

He bumped into Poh at the top as another salvo of sparks illuminated the space around them.

SPARK.

They were in a room with walls once again covered in carvings of elephants.

SPARK.

They could see nothing else in the darkness.

SPARK. SPARK.

"There!" Sam said, shuffling away.

"You see the Gear?"

"No," Sam said. "But something." He bumped into Poh in the dark and passed him what he found.

"A stick?"

"A torch," Sam said, "light it."

SPARK. SPARK.

The room lit up with a warm glow. The heavy wooden staff was bound at the top with wax and coconut palm fibres.

It's OK. It's just a small fire.

"Argh!" Sam startled back.

"What is it?"

"Something just ran over my foot!" Sam said.

"Let me see," Poh said, moving around with the torch and sweeping it close to the floor. "Oh, it's just a spider."

"Just a spider!" Sam watched the huge, black hairy spider walk away from the firelight. "That thing could eat a bird!"

"They do," Poh said. "Though I'd say in here he's probably eating bats."

"Great, just great," Sam muttered. "Pass me the torch!"

Sam led the way through the room. The orange firelight cast long shadows, lighting a small area around them and not much else. The molten wax dripped to the floor and left tiny little fires in their wake as they walked, as though they were leaving behind a trail of burning candles.

"Wait," Sam said, stopping. Poh stood next to him. "Look. Just up ahead."

They took a small step forward, then another.

Poh looked up. "Wow."

Sam followed his gaze.

A huge stone statue stood before them.

"Is that what I think it is?" Sam said.

"Yes."

"OK, wow." There was no mistaking it. "That's a giant elephant's butt right there."

The two of them laughed as they moved around the larger-than-life stone elephant.

"And look at all the bling," Sam said.

"Bling?"

"All those jewels and stuff," Sam said, walking around it. Inset into the stone were an uncountable amount of shiny gems.

"I've heard of this!" Poh said. "The jewelled elephant. I thought it was just make-believe, a story told to children."

"It's no myth." They neared the front of the elephant. The tusks were ringed with bracelets of gold. The trunk was stacked with necklaces made of gold and jewels. "I'm guessing this is the biggest elephant that you've seen?"

"Yes," Poh said, smiling, reaching up and running his hand along the curve of the elephant's trunk and then through the dangling chains. "I am so surprised that the happy dream, the story that my mother used to tell me, is really true."

"But?" Sam asked, flinching as a bit of hot wax and material from the fire torch hit his hand.

"My dream was really for this," Poh said, holding a shiny disk in his hand, the centre of it looped through a chain around the elephant's neck. He unclasped it, and Sam held the torch closer.

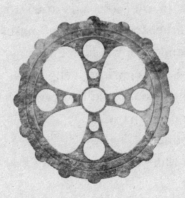

"That's it!"

The room shook slightly.

"Did you feel that?" Sam asked, standing rock-still.

"Ah, Sam," Poh said, looking at the elephant, then at the pedestal that it—and they—stood upon. "I do not think we should have stood here."

Sam looked down at his feet. There was the sound of creaking and whining, the sound of something set in motion. Then the giant stone pedestal started to lower to the ground level.

"We have to get out of here!" Sam said.

Poh tucked the Gear into his waistband and they ran for the top of the staircase.

There was a bone-shaking rumble before them and then a grinding noise of something massive moving in the dark.

A slab of stone had slid down, smashing shut with a crunch and enclosing the doorway and sealing them in the chamber.

Sam went to the door and tried to move it. The edges, like all the stonework of the Angkor complex, was practically seamless. It would not push nor pull nor lift in the slightest. Sam knew from banging on the stone door that it was thick and would be heavier than a car. They would not be able to move it.

They were trapped.

What is it with me and getting stuck in rooms all of a sudden?

"We're not getting out this way," Sam said. "Time to find a plan B." He passed the torch back to Poh. "Can you guide us with some light?"

"Yes," Poh replied, taking the light. "But do you . . . do you hear that?"

Sam paused and wrestled to control his breathing which was loud and fast. He was too spooked to hear anything at first.

"Yes, I can hear it," Sam said, and he swallowed hard.

It was water—running fast and getting louder.

ALEX

Alex stood outside on the rear deck. His head was bandaged tight. Looking over the side, he could see the massive dent in the ship's thick metal side where the second missile had struck. In places, small holes let water in, and he knew that the *Ra*'s pumps were working overtime to keep the sea water out as they limped to the nearest port for repairs.

The worst damage was to the forward deck.

Alex looked up ahead and saw the charred and blackened bow, steel twisted and broken from a direct hit.

Dawn was just beginning to break directly behind them. That meant that they were headed west—the *Ra* had changed direction in the night.

Where are we headed now?

The weather had turned too, the sea today a rough ride as the *Ra*'s mighty hull cut through it at full speed.

He was afraid of the water—of drowning. He always had been. He remembered the helicopter crash-landing in the pool, when he'd first met Sam and Eva. But now, as he gripped the handrail and felt at one with the yacht as it ploughed through the waves, he felt hopeful.

This is my destiny. I have to face my own fears to fulfil it.

Alex watched as the orange-red glow grew to a sliver of bright yellow that glinted off the tops of waves and seemed, as though through some intervention into the cosmic order of things, to calm the swell.

"Early riser," Hans said. He joined Alex at the handrail. His left arm was in a sling and there was stitching across his forehead holding an angry and swollen cut together. "Couldn't sleep?"

Alex gave him a questioning look.

"Yes, Alex," Hans said, "I remember the dream."

"We're going to Antarctica," Alex said. "But now we're headed west."

"True," Hans said, looking at the horizon. "We must stop and make repairs. And we need a hospital to scan that head of yours. Can't have a last 13 Dreamer with a couple of screws loose, can we?"

Alex almost laughed.

"Are you still feeling seasick?"

"Not as much as I'd thought," Alex said.

"Well, you'll get some respite today," Hans replied. "We'll be on dry land for a while."

"Where?"

"The Marshall Islands."

"What's there?" Alex asked.

"Not much, but to the west of there is something my

grandfather always wanted to see but never got the chance."

"Sounds mysterious," Alex said.

"You have no idea."

Alex looked out at the water. Out of habit, he clung onto the railing as he looked at the rise and fall of the waves. He looked down at his hands and let go. He stood there, taking the ride through his legs, and looked out at the sea with a new determination.

"Do we have time for this sightseeing trip?" Alex asked.

"Ah. Well, actually, no. But I think it's vital. My grandfather always talked to me about this place, and as I fell asleep last night I heard him telling me 'go there!'."

"So you're a Dreamer too."

"Either that or I have a good imagination," Hans grimaced. "I was never blessed with the Dreaming capabilities of others. But I found other ways to make up for that shortfall . . ."

Do I sense some Dreamer envy here?

Alex wisely chose to simply nod and shrug.

Hans let the topic drop and patted Alex on the back. "Follow me, I'll show you."

Alex followed Hans into the ship, and through to his office, on the level below the main deck, at the stern. The back wall had wrap-around windows that looked out to the ship's wake.

"Look here," Hans said, bringing up an image on a large wall-mounted screen. "Do you know the zodiac?"

"I know that I'm a Taurus," Alex laughed.

"Right. Well, maybe, maybe not. The dates most people know are actually incorrect. And you're talking about astrology. *I'm* talking from an astronomical point of view. Here, if we count all the traditional constellations, there are thirteen in the zodiac, not twelve."

"Really?"

"Really. Rather than a neat thirty degrees, they're—ah, it's complicated."

"Try me."

"Well, it is important to distinguish the zodiac symbols we all know—Aries, Gemini and so on—from the actual constellations associated with them. The constellations are not even, not so conveniently divided up in the cosmos."

"OK, I get that. We've divided the zodiac neatly, but in reality, by the constellations, they're different sizes."

Hans nodded.

"So here are the dates, give or take one day each year," Hans said, changing images on the touch screen, "when the Sun is between Earth and each of these thirteen constellations."

"Huh. That makes me an Aries," Alex said. "Thirteen constellations, eh?"

"That's right. The constellation boundaries were redefined in 1930, listing the twelve traditional zodiac constellations plus Ophiuchus. It comes in between Scorpio and Sagittarius."

CONSTELLATION	DATES	DAYS
Sagittarius	Dec 18 - Jan 18	32
Capricornus	Jan 19 - Feb 15	28
Aquarius	Feb 16 - Mar 11	24
Pisces	Mar 12 - Apr 18	38
Aries	Apr 19 - May 13	25
Taurus	May 14 - Jun 19	37
Gemini	Jun 20 - Jul 20	31
Cancer	Jul 21 - Aug 9	20
Leo	Aug 10 - Sep 15	37
Virgo	Sep 16 - Oct 30	45
Libra	Oct 31 - Nov 22	23
Scorpius	Nov 23 - Nov 29	7
Ophiuchus	Nov 30 - Dec 17	18

"Ophiuchus?" Alex said. "Never heard of it. I'm guessing because it would clash with our thoughts of thirty-day zodiacs, give or take."

"Correct."

"So what's this mean for *us?*"

"The Bakhu Machine is designed to work as a mechanical map, and according to da Vinci's journal it will show us where to go via reading the stars in the sky. But his notes reveal it will only give a location during the thirteenth sign, Ophiuchus."

"But that only goes from November thirtieth to mid-December. That's like," Alex counted furiously, "only an eighteen-day window. That means . . ."

Hans nodded. "If we miss it, we must wait another year."

Alex looked at the image of the Ophiuchus constellation scanned from da Vinci's sketch.

This is happening fast. I gotta tell the Enterprise and Academy. Does Sam know there's so little time left?

Then he wondered how his dream would come to him.

Will I be aware of it? Will I know I'm dreaming and that nothing can really harm me? Where will it lead me?

"It sets our deadline," Hans said. "It gives us that window, and no more."

Looks like we haven't got long to save the world.

SAM

WHOOSH!

Water began to flood the chamber. It was a torrent, flowing from a square water pipe set into a wall above their heads.

By the light of Poh's still-burning torch, Sam could see that the room had no other exits.

"There's no way out that I can see!" Sam said. He felt around, the walls all carved with reliefs, but solid. The only way in and out, it seemed, was flooded with water. "Did this happen in your dream?"

Poh fell silent and seemed dumbstruck for a moment, now pointlessly holding the Gear above his head, the water now halfway up their shins. Sam took the torch from him and continued searching around the walls.

"Poh, what happened in your dream? Were we trapped like this?"

"No," Poh said, his voice now calm. "But I think I know a way out."

"Where?" Sam asked, sloshing over, the water now at his knees.

"Somewhere . . ." Poh replied, moving to the wall opposite the water drain where they'd entered.

The water was now over Sam's knees—at this rate it would fill the room in two minutes.

"Poh?"

"This elephant here," Poh said.

Sam held the torch closer to light the frieze before them. He couldn't see that the elephant carving was different to any of the others.

"There is a door," Poh said. "Hold this."

Sam took the Gear, looping it onto his dreamcatcher necklace so that he could continue to provide light as Poh felt around the stonework before them. The water was at their thighs.

"Higher," Poh said.

"Sorry?"

"We have to wait until the water takes us higher," Poh said.

"You're sure?"

"Yes. Higher."

Sam didn't like it, but he trusted his new friend. They waited for a full minute until the water was under their armpits, and soon after Sam was on tiptoes, then he was floating up off the floor.

He kicked his feet, struggling to keep the torch above the water, then he remembered his Stealth Suit. He changed it, inflating it like a life vest around his chest.

Sam felt for the Gear around his neck, worried that it would sink if the necklace broke. He held the torch over his head and—

"Hang onto me," he said.

Poh didn't answer. He grinned down from above Sam. He'd used the rising water to take him up onto a ledge.

"Take my hand!" Poh said.

Sam reached up and first passed over the torch, then his hand and was pulled up and out of the water onto a ledge where he sat and caught his breath. He changed his Stealth Suit back to a T-shirt and shorts.

The water seemed to stop its flood at their feet, draining out somewhere. There was just enough room for them to sit on the ledge, the ceiling just centimetres above their heads.

"Look!" Sam said. What at first had seemed an illusion in the stone above, was actually those same initials carved into a stone paver, identical to the one that they had used to access the tunnel earlier. "Let's try it."

It took Sam and Poh ten minutes to work the stone free just enough so it moved a few millimetres.

"Great," Sam said, utterly exhausted. "There's probably a tree grown over the top of it."

"Sorry," Poh said. "That was a neat trick with your clothes," he added. "Your shirt turned inflatable—that must be expensive clothing."

"Yeah." Sam watched the flame flicker. Then suddenly he grinned. "Poh—you're a genius!"

Let's hope this newer Suit works better than the last time I tried this.

Sam changed the Stealth Suit so that it had long sleeves, then he pulled some of the memory fabric to cover his right hand, and pressed it under the tiny gap that they'd managed to make in the paver above.

"Watch out," Sam said, then he changed the fabric again—this time in an ever-expanding mass at the point where it covered his hand, so that, slowly, it formed an air-filled jack pushing up against the paving stone.

CREAK.

EVA

Eva sat down on the steps of the Eiffel Tower, exhausted. In the last two hours, she estimated she'd gone through at least twenty doors, each time finding herself confronted by a sinister presence. Each time she'd had to keep running.

I can't believe this is how the construct is meant to work. I'm going to have a heart attack from all this running and stressing out. Man, where are you, Zara and Xavier?

"Eva! Eva!"

At first she thought she was imagining her name being called out on the wind. She stood up and spun around, searching the crowds for a familiar face.

In the sea of faces, she saw one, but not one she was expecting.

Imena!

She was pushing through the crowd, her team members coming up behind her.

So what's the protocol here? Do I fight them, run from them or help them?

Then Eva noticed Imena was limping badly and she ran toward her. "What happened, are you OK?"

"We must get out of here," Imena gasped, almost collapsing into Eva's open arms.

"OK, let me wait for my team and we'll find a white door," Eva said.

"No! We need to get out of here *completely*. The construct, it—they keep coming, almost every door, white, black, it doesn't matter," one of her teammates cried out.

They look scared to death.

"Something is wrong," Imena said. "The construct is created from my mind but there are things in here that should not be. Bad things, *dark* things."

"Something has been chasing me too but I thought maybe it was part of the competition," Eva replied.

"There is a black door not far from here," one of the North-East team said. "We must go through and get out of the construct."

The three of them began to move toward the east leg of the Tower, but Eva hung back.

I can't just leave without them.

"No, I have to warn Zara and Xavier, I don't know if they—" but she never finished her sentence.

The sky filled with darkness, and as the others screamed and started running, Eva could see men in black coming toward them, pushing the crowd aside, guns drawn.

We're out of time.

Eva sprinted with the others to the black door in the east base of the Tower, gunshots ringing out around her, screams filling the air.

Just as she reached the door, she felt a hand on her arm—grasping, pulling her back.

"Get off of me!" she yelled as she swung around and punched her attacker in the jaw. The assassin reeled, caught off guard.

Eva did not hesitate. She threw herself through the open black doorway, following the others.

Think of home, think of waking up, think of being out of here.

But Eva did not wake up.

SAM

"Do you know where we are?" Sam asked, getting to his feet at the top of what looked like a raised stone structure. Their torch had now burned out but by the light of the full moon he could see that they were still in the Angkor complex, but somewhere he'd not seen before.

"Yes!" Poh said. "We are in Angkor Thom, above the Terrace of the Elephants!"

"Of course we are," Sam smiled. He helped Poh put the paver back over the hole, and then followed Poh around and down a set of stairs. He paused to look back at a wall of impressively carved elephants. This time, they were not carved like a drawing onto the stone, they were carved *out* of it, their enormous trunks forming columns. In the moonlight, it looked like a wall of elephants walking toward them.

"This terrace was used by Angkor's kings as a platform from which to view the victorious returning armies."

"And our camp?" Sam asked. For all the trees, he could see no light from their camp fire.

"South of here, follow me," Poh said.

"Tobias?" Sam called out as he and Poh finally came to where they'd set up camp. It was immediately apparent that something was wrong. The camp fire was out, its embers a dull glow. Tobias and the elephant were gone. "Tobias!"

There was no answer to Sam's call.

"Dara?" Poh said, holding up a stake with torn rope hanging from it. "She must have gotten scared—she ran east, to the forest!"

Sam looked up in the direction that Poh pointed. There was no noise from there, but there were clear signs of disturbance on the ground that gave away the elephant's path.

Sam could see that the stones that they'd placed as a little windbreak around the fire had been knocked over. "Maybe Tobias chased after her," he said, "and he kicked out the fire in a rush before he left."

"I must go and get her," Poh said. "I will bring her back."

"OK," Sam replied. "I'll wait here, in case Tobias returns to the camp."

Poh nodded and ran off.

Sam knelt at the dying embers and swept them into a pile, adding some of the dried branches that they'd collected earlier. The fire spat and crackled and the camp site was gradually illuminated some more. Near the fire, a glint caught Sam's eyes. He moved over and picked up a shiny brass object.

A bullet casing.

He looked around the fire and immediately found three more. They had not been there before.

Something terrible has happened here.

"Sam?"

Sam fell over from his crouch with a start. "Tobias?" he called out into the dark.

Suddenly Tobias appeared before Sam. He'd had his Stealth Suit turn invisible, and was not three metres from the fire, lying on the ground. He'd been trying to hide from whoever had been here before, shooting.

It had not been enough.

Tobias was clutching at his stomach. Sam could see instantly that he'd been wounded very badly.

"What happened?" Sam said, kneeling down to his friend and mentor, cradling his head in his arms.

"Poachers, robbers maybe. They jumped me. I'm sorry . . ."

"We have to get you to a hospital," Sam said.

"No."

"Yes, I'm sure—"

"No, Sam," Tobias said quietly.

"I'm going to—"

"Sam, no. It's too late." Tobias looked up at him and smiled weakly. "This is it."

"No, it can't be. Not like this . . ."

"Yes."

Sam fell silent. He checked under Tobias' clutched hands and found a terrible gunshot wound. His friend, his teacher, had only minutes to live.

Tears started to roll down Sam's face.

36

ALEX

Just as dawn broke into a brilliant day, the *Ra* docked at the Marshall Islands. Alex was taken to a local hospital, where he was diagnosed with a slight concussion. Afterwards, Alex, Hans and Ahmed, along with two guards, boarded a chartered helicopter and went west to nearby Micronesia while the ship was repaired and took on supplies and fuel.

"How long?" Alex asked. "Until we set off again, I mean?"

"We'll be back before sunset," Hans said. "The *Ra* should be shipshape by then."

Alex nodded.

Should I go? When we get back to the Marshall Islands, should I slip away, and call for the Enterprise to pick me up? This is too crazy now, right?

The flight took them over deep water and then the crystalline blue waters around sand and coral cays. Ahmed whooped with joy, laughing and pointing out the window at the natural beauty below.

The pilot slowed the helicopter to a hover near a little wooden jetty dotted with local fishermen and dozens of little boats. They headed toward a stretch of sand next to it. Alex winced as the helicopter touched down on the white sand, the shallow crystal blue water lapping over the landing skids.

"We practically landed on the water!" Ahmed said. "We flew through the air and landed on water. How magnificent!"

Hans laughed too, although he saw that Alex looked a little green around the gills. "What's wrong?" Hans asked him.

"Just recalling the last time I was on a helicopter and came down on water," Alex said, thinking again of that splashdown in the backyard pool all those weeks ago.

Feels like years.

It took Hans' guards two minutes to hire them a fishing boat with a crew to take them out to sea. Alex saw a thick wad of cash handed to the crew, who seemed to be a very untrustworthy-looking group of men.

Great, now I'm in a pirate movie.

Alex was in a life vest, sitting on the stern deck, the motion of the boat and the smell of fish guts and engine exhaust fumes making him nauseated.

"It won't be long," Hans said to Alex and clapped him on the back. "It's just a short boat ride around the island."

Alex nodded.

"You are smart, Alex. You will be a great leader, you know that?" Hans said. "A worthy member of the last 13."

"There are only four left to be found," Alex said. "I'm still not convinced I'm one of them."

Hans shook his head. "No. There's three left. They are headed to the fourth right now."

"They are?" Alex was surprised.

"Yes."

"How do you know that?"

"I have eyes and ears everywhere."

"Spies?"

"People who work for me, yes."

"Then why don't you go and get that Gear, then?"

"Because no one else is looking for *this* one, your Gear, and when it's time, we'll already be there. We will find it first."

"In Antarctica?" Alex was skeptical.

"I think so."

"How?"

Hans wouldn't answer, but Alex could see that there was something there.

"What is it?" Alex said. "What aren't you telling me?"

Hans sighed. "We've tracked your dreams your whole life, Alex. Yours and many others. The Eiffel Tower, the Washington Monument—all those towers the Academy and Enterprise so willingly overlooked. They've been operational all along."

"What?" Alex couldn't hide his shock.

"Even the Space Needle in Seattle, ha!" Hans looked

pleased with himself.

So all that messing about at the Monument was for nothing?

Alex forced himself to focus. "So what?" he said. "What are you saying?"

"You dream of Antarctica a lot."

"No I don't," Alex said. "I never have."

"You have, and you continue to," Hans replied. "It's a type of dream you do not remember when you wake up. If you had stayed at the Academy as a student, studying as others have had the chance to, they would have taught you how to recall and master such dreams. You could have reached your full Dreamer potential."

"So what are you saying? That I've had all these dreams of Antarctica that I can't remember and that means I have to go there?"

"Yes," Hans said. "These type of dreams are linked to destiny."

Alex didn't know what to say. He sat in silence, watching as they passed by tropical islands. Ahmed sat at the prow, taking it all in. The Guardians watched the boat's crew, eyeing them cautiously.

"If I'm really linked to this Gear," Alex said, "I'll be one of the last three left." Alex leaned against the railing behind his back and watched the sea. A pod of dolphins jumped in and out of the ship's wake, doing their best to keep up, but the craft was going too fast. The seasickness tablet he'd had was starting to wear off and he felt the rising nausea overwhelming him.

"Everyone else is so sure that I am something," Alex said, "it's starting to freak me out."

Hans stood next to him, watching the view of the island passing by.

"And even if I do turn out to be the Dreamer people say I am," Alex said, "who's to say that I will even be able to do what's *expected* of me? What's *needed* of me?"

"You think Sam does not have such doubts?" Hans was quiet, then added, "It is natural to have doubt, Alex."

"I don't know what Sam thinks, or how he copes," Alex said. "I've hardly seen him since all this started."

"Well, I have seen him, and heard about him, and he's exactly like you—they all are," Hans said. "None of this is easy for anyone involved."

Alex looked to Hans. His bald head was shiny in the sun. His pale blue eyes, his almost total lack of eyebrows or eyelashes, his thin mouth—it had all been a little off-putting at first but now he seemed almost like a slightly crazy but jovial uncle.

"If you didn't feel apprehensive about your abilities and what lies ahead of you," Hans said, "I would be worried."

"Why?"

Hans looked at him.

"Because, Alex, if you are too confident you will make mistakes," he said. "I have the resources and manpower to put to many tasks, but I am always nervous when the stakes are high. Being afraid to fail is a healthy thing. It keeps you sharp. It keeps you determined. It steels your nerves and focuses you. Don't ever forget that."

Abruptly Hans stood up straighter, squinting at the shore. Then he pointed, "There! It's there!"

37

SAM

"Where's your phone?" Sam asked. "Tobias, where is it? I'll call for help."

"They took it," Tobias replied. "The elephant—it ran off and they chased it. Did you find the Gear?"

Sam was silent.

"Sam?"

"Yes, we found it."

"Good. Now, Sam, listen to me," Tobias said, rasping for breath. "If Solaris or another dark force gets the power at the end of this, beyond the Dream Gate, it will plunge the world into total darkness. You—you *must* succeed. You must . . ."

"I will," Sam said, tears in his eyes. "I promise."

"Sam, your fear, of fire . . . you know the evil that exists within Solaris, and he knows your fear. That's why his weapon is fire, do you see?"

Sam nodded.

"My job in your life has been to help you understand and manage your fear. You can fight him, Sam. You can fight him and win."

"Please, Tobias—"

"We all experience fear," Tobias said. "Mine, growing up, was a fear of being alone. Duke helped me through that. I hope that I did that for you. At least I managed to do that . . ."

"Please, Tobias, don't go . . . don't leave me," Sam couldn't see through his tears, wiping them away with his sleeve.

Tobias put a hand to Sam's face and looked up at him. "I know I shouldn't have, but in some ways I thought of you as the son I never had the chance to have." Tobias' breathing came slowly now. "Be strong, Sam, I know you can be. Believe in yourself, like I believe in you."

"I will," Sam whispered, clutching Tobias to him, cradling his head gently.

"And don't be sorry about what happened. I'm not. I chose this destiny." Tobias grasped Sam's hand and squeezed it tight.

"You're the bravest person I've ever known," Sam said. "I love you, Tobias."

Tobias smiled and closed his eyes.

"Just hang in there, please? I'll call for help. We'll get you help . . ." Sam's desperation rang through the still night.

Tobias was silent. Still.

"Tobias?" Sam said quietly.

There was no answer.

He was gone.

"Noooo!" Sam's cries rose into the dark—long, gasping

cries that shuddered through his body as he tried to absorb the pain in his heart.

Poh ran back into the clearing to find Sam holding Tobias' body and staring at the dancing flames of the fire as tears streamed down his face.

EVA

All Eva could hear was the rushing wind. From where she lay on the ground, huddled up in a ball, it tore at her, cold and menacing.

Where am I?

Eva opened her eyes and forced herself to sit up, looking around as she tried to stand in the howling gale.

She reeled from shock as she realized she was standing on a tiny patch of ground, no bigger than a small front yard—but this lawn was way up high, higher than the highest mountain she'd ever seen. She knew she shouldn't, but she just had to look over the edge.

Her panic attack came swiftly and threatened to overwhelm her as she cried out in horror. She was miles up in the sky, only dark clouds above, the ground a hazy grey below.

It isn't real! I'm in my worst nightmare. I have to fight it!

"Eva."

Solaris' voice trickled through the air. It was scratchy and metallic, projecting itself right into Eva's skull. "Come out and play, Eva . . ."

This is just a dream. I can control it. Steer it. Come on!

WHOOSH!

A ball of flame shot past her, streaming through the air.

"Is that it? Is that all you've got?" Eva screamed in defiance. Her voice sounded pitiful in the fury of the gale. She stood with her fists clenched, slowly inching back to the edge.

I have to die to get out of here. The only choice I have now is how.

She looked down again, forcing herself to square off at the very edge.

"Oh, so you're a tough girl?" Solaris laughed, the evil sound echoing mercilessly around her. "Go on then, jump! Are you sure you'll wake up?"

What? He can't have changed that. Can he?

The ground shook, sending Eva stumbling backwards. The grass beneath her feet was moving. No, it was *shrinking*.

Within moments, Eva had only the smallest patch of earth to stand on, a pinnacle reaching up endlessly—her worst nightmare come true.

"No! This can't be!" she screamed, wobbling dangerously as she struggled to keep her balance.

"Who's the brave one now?" Solaris said. "Thought you could beat me? Thought you could *win?*" Malice dripped from every word.

"You'll never win!" she screamed. "You coward!"

Eva jumped.

Eva was suddenly more awake than she'd ever been. She sat upright in her reclining chair, gasping for breath, hearing the applause from the crowd and then a sudden hush fell over them.

She spun around to see Zara coughing and fighting for air in the chair next to her but waved away the medical staff. She'd clearly just forced her way out of the construct too. Zara turned to Eva, her eyes wide.

"Dark, it was so dark . . . I didn't think I—you . . . is it over?" she stuttered.

"Me too," Eva said, shaking as she leaned over to grasp Zara's hand. "I wanted to warn you but they came for me. I should have found you and Xavier—"

Instinctively, they turned to Xavier.

He wasn't moving at all.

"What?" Eva asked, getting out of her chair and pulling the electrode stickers off her temples. "What's wrong with him?"

"We don't know," the chief medic said, his face and voice full of concern. "But his pulse is too low—we're losing him!"

"Whatever they've done to the construct, it's left him in there too deep!" Lora said to the medic. "He's stuck in the dream!"

"Clear!" the medic yelled, and all staffers took a step back as—

WHAM!

The defibrillator paddles sparked to life against Xavier's chest.

It's not working! He's going to die!

"Clear!" the medic called again.

WHAM!

The defibrillator shook Xavier's body.

"He's not waking up!" Eva yelled.

SAM

Sam was in New York City again.

Memories of his first mission there—to retrieve the Star of Egypt and the key hidden within it—swirled in his mind. As did the memory of Sebastian's death at the hands of Stella, shot from the sky in the Academy jet.

More recent memories from two nights ago in Cambodia pushed their way through. He had found it almost impossible to sleep since then. He feared the nightmares that would come. The thought of Tobias not being in his life anymore seemed too much to bear. As hard as that fact was in his waking life, Sam knew the pain might be even worse in his dreams.

The sunrise glinted off the windows of the hotel opposite as there was a knock at the door. Sam opened it.

"We leave in half an hour," the Professor said. "I just wanted to make sure you were awake."

"More than I've ever been," Sam replied. He could see security personnel down the hallway—Secret Service, NYPD and a lot of men and women in suits. All of them there to protect him.

Who will protect the others? Who will protect the world?
Me.

"Are you OK?" the Professor asked as they stepped back into the room.

Sam nodded. "I—I miss him. Tobias. Can I do this without him?"

"Yes. It is what he would want," the Professor replied.

"The funeral is tomorrow?"

"Yes."

Sam looked out at the view.

"The world will change once you speak this morning," the Professor said. "You know that, don't you?

Sam nodded.

"Have you worked out what you are going to say?"

He nodded again.

"Sam?" the Professor persisted.

"Yes," he said. "Sorry, Professor. I'm just a bit exhausted."

"I'll get you some breakfast, you go shower and get ready," the Professor said.

Sam smiled. "Thanks."

"No. Thank you, Sam. We're all thankful, for everything." The Professor hugged him. "I'm so sorry about Tobias. I know how much he meant to you. Please believe we are sharing your pain. I knew him from . . . anyway, today is not the day to speak of this. But there will be other times to remember him."

"I know," Sam replied, choking back his emotions. It was

all still too raw. "Any word from the others? From Alex?"

"Just before," the Professor replied. "Jedi received a message. Seems Alex is making a stop in the Pacific. And he has learned of a countdown."

"Countdown?"

"Something I've suspected, and Alex, via Dr. Kader, has confirmed."

"Yes?"

"The thirteenth zodiac, Sam," the Professor said. "That's our deadline."

"Oh, wow. So should I be making more notes here?" Sam said as he pulled out some small pieces of paper.

"How about I brief you over breakfast?" the Professor smiled gamely.

"Sure," Sam replied. "I'm definitely open to your advice."

"Just be yourself up there," the Professor said.

40

ALEX

Alex could not believe his eyes.

What at first seemed a rocky mangrove estuary turned out to be a city made of stone. They were no longer navigating through mangrove growth but canals. An ancient city made of huge stone slabs surrounded them, all of it aged and covered in overgrowth, hinting at how old and long deserted it was.

From the fishing boat, Alex, Hans, Ahmed and one of the Guardians had transferred into a smaller tin dingy with just one fisherman at the helm. The tiny boat slipped almost silently through the incredible landscape.

"This is Nan Madol," Hans said. "A ruined city that was once the capital of the Saudeleur dynasty, until about five hundred years ago."

Alex took in the city as they travelled the winding canals, Ahmed at the helm next to the fisherman, pointing and constantly checking a map. At least a hundred artificial islets were bordered by the tidal canals.

"This is incredible," Alex said.

"The name Nan Madol means 'spaces between,'" Hans

said, "and is a reference to the canals that criss-cross the ruins. It is often called the Venice of the Pacific."

"And what is it we're looking for?" Alex asked.

"That," Ahmed said, pointing to the square mouth of a canal, overhung with a roof. "That is it!"

Inside the cave-like tunnel, by the light from the single flashlight from Ahmed's pack, Alex was surprised at how small and unadorned it all was. It was made from simple slabs of black stones stacked one upon another, much like a log cabin. There was no indication of any decoration or carvings. Looking back, he saw the glow outside from where they had tied their boat to a small stone pier, the Guardian keeping watch.

"Go back and bring more flashlights," Hans called to him. "And make sure those fishermen wait for us."

The Guardian headed off without a word.

"Well, this is cosy," Alex said, his voice echoing in the dark stone confines.

"Follow me," Ahmed replied, leading the way with the light. "You can tell from the layout that there is something important this way."

"Really?" Alex said. "You can tell that from looking at these rocks? It all looks the same to me."

"You need a keener eye than that to become an

archaeologist," Ahmed chuckled.

"I guess so." Alex went last, his feet shuffling along in the near darkness as they left the light of the entrance and wound through the ever-darkening maze.

"Wait," Ahmed said, and the three of them stopped. The Egyptologist doubled back, running his fingers along the dusty stone wall. "Here, look."

Alex saw an inscription on the wall. It showed a faint carving—a picture of a pyramid. Ahmed took a small brush from his pack and cleaned it off.

"I've seen that image somewhere before," Alex said.

"It's called the Eye of Providence," Ahmed replied. "You probably know it from the back of a an American one-dollar bill."

"And what's it doing carved into this wall in the middle of nowhere?" Alex asked.

"We'll soon find out," Hans said.

They waited while Dr. Kader took a wax rubbing of the carving in his notebook.

"This way," he said, leading them on with the flashlight.

"Here's another one," Alex said twenty paces later. He'd been running his hand along the stone and felt the same carving at the same height. By the glow of the flashlight, he saw the same thirteen-level pyramid.

"They're markers," Ahmed said, "made by Guardians."

"Guardians?"

"Yes, I've seen similar markings in other monuments in other countries," Ahmed said. "The Egyptian Guardians must have been through here, judging by the state of these carvings. Maybe a hundred years or more ago."

"Why would they come here?" Alex asked.

"Because they were searching for the Gate," Hans said. "Or anything related to it."

"The Egyptian Guardians take their duty seriously," Ahmed said.

Yeah, I know.

The next marker was at a junction and this one was different. This pyramid was on its side, pointing like an arrow. Ahmed led them around to the left, where it opened up into a chamber but it proved to be a dead end.

Inside the chamber it was pitch black. Water dripped from the ceiling into a pool where the echo of the droplets suggested that the room was an enormous cavern.

"Should we wait for more light?" Alex said. "For the Guardian to return?"

"No," Hans replied, taking the flashlight from Ahmed

and walking ahead.

Alex kept close behind.

The far wall was different to the others. For a start, Alex could see it was smooth. Smooth and carved with very faint but deliberate lines.

"A true artist made this," Ahmed said, using a small paintbrush from his pack to clean off the lines. "Such detail . . ."

"This is the map room," Hans said, holding the flash-light steady as Ahmed worked. "A map of the world made in the 1500s."

"So what?" Alex said. "We've got real maps these days, accurate, made by GPS and satellites, you know."

"This was made before all the continents were even known," Ahmed said, "but look."

Alex looked at where Ahmed was now cleaning—the southern-most continent, Antarctica.

"Well, it's guesswork," Alex said. "They knew land was down there, but they'd obviously not been there, right?"

"Why do you say that?" Hans asked as Ahmed took a wax rubbing of the map.

"Because that looks nothing like Antarctica!" Alex said.

"It does, Alex," Hans said. "Just not Antarctica as we know it today."

"Huh?"

"This map is based on ancient maps and knowledge," Hans said.

"How ancient?"

"Perhaps from before the last ice age."

"What are you saying?" Alex asked.

"What we're saying, Alex, is that just like the other old maps we have, this shows Antarctica before it had ice covering the land mass."

"But that's—"

"Impossible?" Hans said. "No. Improbable, sure. But no more improbable than this stone city on a tiny Pacific island. Or teenagers having dreams of Gears lost to time. History, and our world, is an incredible place, Alex—"

A gunshot rang out. The sound echoed around the chamber, buffeting them from all sides.

"Where did that come from?" Ahmed whispered, rolling up his wax rubbing and tucking it into his pack.

"I'm not sure," Hans said, taking a dart gun from his belt. "We should go—"

"Wait!" Alex said. "Listen!"

There was the thrum of an engine, growing louder, then a bang rang out and the engine noise returned.

"The boat has come back, that's all," Ahmed said. "It's just the old engine playing up."

"No matter, let's go!" Hans said, leading them out at a run.

"No!" Alex called out from behind them. "Something's not right!"

The three of them stopped. Alex pointed toward the

dull glow of the entry, and he followed the light and the engine noise. They slowed to a walk, wary.

The Guardian was there in the boat. But he'd clearly not been to get more supplies. He was slumped over the outboard, unconscious, the engine still at full throttle and the bow pushing hard up against the rocks.

"I have a feeling that we're in trouble," Alex said, stopping his advance.

Hans patted Alex on the shoulder and pointed into the shadows near the mouth of the entrance, an area visible from this angle but not when they entered earlier. A camouflaged net had been covering it.

There were crates stacked up there—dozens of them. There were weapons too, boxes of ammunition, stacks of grenades, along with all kinds of electrical items, communications gear, audio-visual equipment—a bounty of looted goods.

"What *is* all this?" Alex asked as the three of them inched closer.

"Pirates," Hans said, worried. "They must have been using this place to hide their stolen goods and weapons. We have to get out of here."

Real pirates!

Alex heard noises to their right. Voices, nearing. "They're here!"

41

SAM

Sam stood in the foyer of the United Nations General Assembly. The American President stood next to him. With them were the British Prime Minister, the Premier of China and the presidents of France and Russia. The five permanent members of the UN Security Council— all there, for him. Supporting him before he walked inside.

And Prime Minister Hashimoto of Japan, who'd arranged this special moment, was right by Sam's side.

"Ready, Sam?" Yutaka asked.

"Yes," he replied.

"Remember," the American President said, "just relax up there—talk to us like we're your friends, like we're here just to hear you."

Sam nodded, feeling anything but confident.

"Pretend that the world is not watching," the Russian President said then laughed and slapped Sam on the back. "You are strong, young Sam. A hero. You will be fine up there."

"Remember," Yutaka said. "Once you finish, we will

address the Assembly, together, to reinforce what you have said. We are all behind you."

The French President smiled at Sam, and his Chinese and British counterparts patted Sam on the back as he walked in.

Sam looked back at Yutaka, who'd managed to persuade the Dreamers among the world leaders to arrange this meeting. He gave him a thumbs up and it actually made Sam choke on a laugh.

Inside the Assembly Hall, the imposing green room somehow reminded Sam a little of the granite Dream Universe room in Japan.

Times about a thousand in size.

The crowd was enormous, far bigger than any school play or other live audience that Sam had ever had to appear before. It was the United Nations General Assembly, representing all one hundred and ninety-three member states.

I'd like to visit them all some day.

The General Secretary made the introduction. "*A special guest speaker . . .*" was all Sam heard.

How many of them know about Dreamers? How many will believe what I have to say?

Sam thought his legs would go out from under him, felt his panic rising.

Then he heard Tobias' voice inside his head, encouraging him, telling him that he was fine, that he'd be OK.

This is my destiny. I was born to do it. It's going to be alright.

Sam took a deep breath and gripped the lectern hard. "Good morning," he said, forcing himself to look up and out into the room, taking in all the eyes upon him.

There was complete silence in the room. Hundreds of faces turned his way, delegates, aides and the press.

All of them watching and listening to me, to what I have to say. Wow.

"I stand before you today," Sam said, "to talk about the terrible plight of the world right now. The world has become gripped by conflict. In some ways this is not new, but I'm here to tell you that there is another reason for what is happening now. It is a terrible time, but I believe we can make it right—all of us, together."

The silence in the room was deafening. Sam was sure that they'd heard such a thing said in this space before. Rhetoric, rallying cries, sound-bites, good intentions— and dreams.

"I stand here today, with you, to tell you a secret," Sam said.

The silence in the room was eerie.

The world is watching me. Listening.

Sam could see several little red lights on the cameras pointed at him, broadcasting and recording his message.

"The secret is what you see before you right now," Sam

said. "The secret is me. Although, I should state, that it's not *just* me—I am not alone."

Sam looked around the room. He took another deep breath and smiled.

This will change the world. Some here would have heard about Dreamers before, or maybe just rumours. But for others, this will be a shock and almost too much to believe.

But, hopefully, many will believe, many will be moved to act, to help, to make a difference.

"I am here to reveal to you today, and to the world at large, the existence of people with special abilities . . ." Sam read from the notes that he'd made in Tobias' little notebook. "I like to think that we are on the precipice of a brave new world. We live in a big, fast-paced, complicated and often scary world. I'm here to tell you that it's all that and more—but there's hope. My name is Sam. I'm a Dreamer—a true Dreamer. One of the last 13. And I'm telling you that our time is now, and that our choice is exactly that—it is *ours.* Today, we can choose to move forward, together, and beat the odds. Or, we take the other path, remain divided, self-interested, and see what becomes of the world."

Silence.

Sam looked over to the six heads of the world's most powerful nations who had encouraged him moments before. They were all there, standing resolute, there for him.

But there's one person who's not here for me anymore. I must make him proud.

"Ladies and gentlemen, citizens of the world . . ." Sam said, looking around the room and then directly at a camera pointed his way. "I'm here to tell you that we have fourteen days left to save the world."